CHAPTER I
The Journey

The year is 1937. Europe is in a state of suspense, with the threat of conflict looming. Adolf Hitler, the German Chancellor, is on the rampage and looking to expand the German State by military means. He has already claimed sections of his neighbours' territory without any resistance, and now seeks further expansion. In another part of Europe, another tyrant is in power, causing death and suffering to his citizens: the country is Russia and its ruler, Joseph Stalin, with his henchmen, rules it with an iron fist, much to the misery of its people, who are continually punished and harassed by the State's secret police, the Peoples' Commissariat for Internal Affairs (NKVD). There is a movement amongst certain groups of people who have the vision of what the future might be, and so are emigrating to countries that they believe will be safer, should a conflict or some other disaster overtake them.

The Aserov family had lived in a small peasant village for three generations, outside the town of Kursk in the Soviet State. Life, for them, had not been too harsh, even with the aggravation by the state or Communist Party village commissars. Today, the family consisted of Aeron Aserov and his wife, Priscilla, both in their fifties. They had a son aged twenty-seven. He was married to a girl who was half Jewish and half Polish Catholic, a talented, intelligent and beautiful woman whose name was Druscilla. She was welcomed into the Aserov household with open arms. Everything in the family's life was harmonious. The

1

parents and the son, whose name was Daniel, had reasonably comfortable houses in comparison to the peasants. Aeron Aserov had qualified as a doctor in Kharkov; he was very much accepted by the local population, especially given that the family was the only Jewish family in the village. The doctor was well known and respected by the locals. He would treat them irrespective of their faith, which was forbidden to be practised in the Soviet Union under penalty of death. His son, Daniel, had also qualified as a doctor, and had a practice in the town of Kursk.

*　*　*

Russia, at this time, was in a grip of terror. The state police, the NKVD, were arresting many of its citizens of professional and intellectual status, along with many Jews and peasants who did not, in the eyes of Stalin's henchmen, obey the state policy. These unfortunates were transported to Siberia or even shot; most of them ended up in camps. Whole families were displaced without any redress or justice. These Siberian slave camps were usually located where the coal and iron was found, and the prisoners' task was to work under Arctic conditions to help the state economy. Although being isolated out in the country, this fact was nevertheless deeply disturbing to the Aserov family, and they were worried this fate could befall them. Daniel, at his practice in the town of Kursk, had been told by one of his patients that there was a purge in progress. The NKVD was targeting all the whole Jewish population and anyone connected to them, even to the extent of taking them away and shooting entire families. Daniel, arriving back home, informed his parents what he had heard, and it frightened him. The family decided to get together and discuss the situation. What should they do? This was deeply disturbing, and a dilemma to which they must find a solution. What could they do, and where would they go? Daniel's father suggested that it would be better to try to

2

Milk & Honey, Blood & Tears

Don Bryne

Raider Publishing International

New York   London

Cover design by Peter Johnston of Johnston Design

ISBN: 978-1-61667-066-5

Published By Raider Publishing International
www.RaiderPublishing.com
New York London Johannesburg
Printed in the United States of America and the United Kingdom

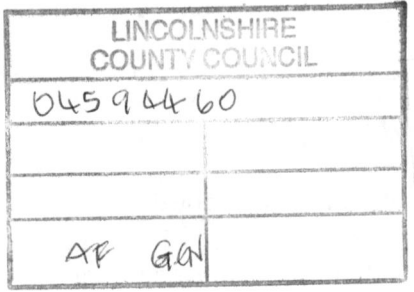

Milk & Honey, Blood & Tears

Don Bryne

get to America, where they would be safe, but how would they all get there? Besides not having passports or other documents, it would be impossible, as a group, to attempt the journey. Somehow, if they wanted to survive, a solution had to be found. Daniel thought that Palestine would, perhaps, be the best place to go; unlike America, it was closer, and it would be possible for them to travel overland if they could stand the journey and avoid the State Police.

*   *   *

The British had a mandate over Palestine at this time, and a large number of Jews had settled there for many generations, and had lived alongside the Palestinians in peaceful co-existence. Aeron, Daniel's father, thought that this would be the best thing to do, if only they could achieve it. The news from Europe was getting worse. France and other countries surrounding Germany were in a state of unease. What might happen if a war was declared by Hitler and the Germans? Britain had made a pact with Hitler, and believed that he had no aggressive designs on his neighbours, which ultimately was not the case. The Aserov family carried on with their work as normal, but kept thinking of a way to leave the country. How would they survive if they decided to leave? How would they get there? These were questions that had to be answered if they wanted to get to Palestine. After a week or so, Daniel and his father, Aeron, got together to discuss what they might do. They came to the conclusion that they should try to get to Palestine; after all, it was, according to the Bible, the Jewish 'Promised Land of milk and honey', so it was a natural desire to want to go there. Having called the family together with their wives, Priscilla and Druscilla— Daniel's wife— they had made up their minds to leave the country, somehow.

The family met again to discuss their dilemma. After considerable thought regarding the logistics of the journey, much to Daniel's surprise, his father said that his wife, Druscilla, and Daniel should go, and leave them behind. He had talked to Priscilla about it, and had thought he— Daniel— and his wife Druscilla would have a better chance of succeeding than if they had all gone together. Besides, he did not want to leave his patients who, with him being the only doctor, relied on him for their health and care. Daniel's father pointed out that he and Priscilla would be all right. Even the NKVD, the State Police, and the village commissars became ill from time to time, so the NKVD would be reluctant to take him away. Aeron assured Daniel that he would survive against the odds, and again pointed out that the state would be foolish to expel or punish a doctor; he believed that even Hitler would exempt a doctor. He would need them if a war were to break out. Daniel, hearing what his father had to say, was torn over what to do. What if he stayed in Russia as a doctor? Would he be treated the same? His mother assured him that they would be all right, and said they should make the journey to Palestine and start a new life, and perhaps, one day, they would be able to join them. If a war started, it would soon be over, as a lesson had been learnt from the 'Great War', and a solution would be found. Although reluctant to leave his family behind, Daniel and Druscilla made arrangements to leave Russia for good. Now, the question was how to go about it. First, Daniel had to think of an excuse to convince his partners at his surgery why he was having time off. He would tell them he had not had a holiday for some time, and that his wife suggested he should take time off, and they would take a trip to the Black Sea coast.

Daniel went to work the next day and said that he would be away for a few days, adding that he was arranging for a Russian doctor to look after his patients. War clouds were looming over Europe. Daniel knew that, if they were going to leave, it really had to be soon. He made arrangements with his father to sell or give his house away after a period of time, to avoid suspicion, and to tell anyone enquiring about his whereabouts that he had perished in an accident, together with his wife, whilst on a journey to the

4

Black Sea. Daniel proceeded to get together what he would need. The family had accumulated a number of valuables, such as gold and silver pieces, over the years. His father suggested he should take as many as he could. It was better than currency, and could be bartered for goods or food. Some of the valuables were worth a considerable amount of money. He may even be able to purchase a house in Palestine with them. Also, they should take enough money for the journey. His father told him to take his 'doctor's credentials' and qualifications, as these would possibly secure him work. It would also be a good idea to take a map of the route they proposed to take. Daniel proceeded to make his arrangements for their departure. He would only take two suitcases, one for him and the other for Druscilla. He would pack them with any clothes they believed would be useful to them, and, hidden in the clothes, they would conceal the valuables. Having done this, Daniel had to make another arrangement with a peasant whom he could trust to take him to Kursk in his horse-drawn carriage or *troika*. For this, he would reward him, and told him the day he would like to travel, telling him also that he would be away for a while taking a holiday to the Black Sea.

* * *

The day came for Daniel and Druscilla to leave. This was to be a very emotional parting; to leave their parents was traumatic and painful. They were setting out on an unknown journey; neither of them had ever left Russia before, and both were full of apprehension. Daniel's father assured him that they would be all right and nothing would befall them, saying that, when he reached Palestine, things in Russia would perhaps change, and they would be able to join them. Saying goodbye to his parents as the *troika* arrived was an emotional occasion. Druscilla burst into tears. Daniel, too, could not keep back his emotions; he loved his parents. They were kind, compassionate and loving, and he knew what a wrench it was to leave them. At the same time, he was thinking about what would be in store for them. However, it was time to leave and, with a last sad farewell, the *troika* trotted off on the dusty road to Kursk.

Arriving at the railway station, Daniel paid the man and thanked him for his services. Then, as he left, the man said he hoped they would have a good holiday, and wished them luck on their journey. At Kursk, they bought two tickets for the train, and waited for it to arrive. It was not long before the train arrived at the draughty station, and Druscilla and Daniel got on board quickly. So far, things were going according to plan, and they settled down for the journey. While the train was at a standstill, a small group boarded the train, two of them in uniform, and two civilians. As the train proceeded on its way, the group worked their way down the carriages questioning passengers. Daniel and Druscilla's hearts jumped with panic. The group were looking very closely at the passengers and asking questions. As they approached, Daniel became more anxious, but the men ignored him and set off further down the carriage. A sigh of relief came over Daniel and Druscilla, and they again settled in their seats, asking a couple of people sitting near them what the men had been looking for. The couple said that it appeared that a prisoner had absconded, and they thought he might be on the train. At the next stop, a small station a few miles down the line, the 'policemen' and the civilians left. The train lurched off and, again, Druscilla and Daniel settled down for the next stop, which was to be Dmepropetrousk.

By this time, they were beginning to feel hungry. They hoped they would be able to find some food at one of the stops. The little food they had brought with them had run out. About an hour later, the train came to a halt at a small station. Hoping he could find some food for them, Daniel left the train, leaving his wife in the carriage. As he was looking around the platform, the train started to move off. Realising the train was moving, panic struck Druscilla's heart. Daniel ran alongside it, and he just managed to pull open one of the doors and climb on board. He was some way down the train, but, eventually, he got to his wife, who was overcome with relief at his return. However, after all that, they still had no food. They were nearing a much larger town and, as they approached it, they thought it must be Dmepropetrousk. Here, at the station, they knew the train would stay for fifteen minutes, and they should be able to get at least some food and a drink. Daniel saw there was a station café, where he was able to purchase some bread, a kind of sausage, and some water. Feeling quite hungry, they soon ate the food and, being a little satisfied, settled down again.

*   *   *

Night had fallen and, after such a traumatic day, coupled with the rocking motion of the train, they both fell asleep. While they both slept, the train passed through the towns of Zaporozhye and Melitopol without stopping. Some time had passed, then, suddenly, the train came to a jolting halt. They were awakened by the jolt and, looking out of the window, could see they had arrived at Sebastopol, the end of their Russian journey.

They got off the train and went out into the street, in the hope of finding somewhere to stay, asking several people who were standing about. At first, no one could help them. Not giving up, Daniel asked a man, a Russian who was advanced in years, if he knew of any place they could stay. The man asked them where they had come from.

Daniel said, "A small village outside Kursk."

The man appeared somewhat surprised to hear this. He replied, "I know that place; I have a brother who lives there. He was very ill, and the local doctor made him better. He is now in good health."

Upon hearing that, Daniel's face lit up, and he told him that his father was the doctor. The man immediately offered to give them a place to stay at his house. They accepted his offer, because they thought it would be safe for them. The man, who had introduced himself as Michael, lived not far from the station, and asked them to follow him. Daniel and Druscilla picked up the suitcases and proceeded with him. The area they arrived at was a little run down, but at least they could rest for the night. The man's house was quite modest; he had few possessions, but he managed to put up a bed in one of the rooms, and made them some soup. Michael asked where they were going. Daniel replied that they were going to stay with some relatives in Turkey. They still wanted to keep their intentions a secret until they felt safe and were out of Russia. After a night's rest, in the morning, at breakfast, Daniel asked Michael if he knew if the ferries went to Istanbul. The man said he believed so, but was not certain. The next morning, wanting to get out of Russia as soon as possible, they said goodbye to Michael and asked him if he wanted payment for his hospitality.

"No," he said; he was very grateful to Daniel's father for making his brother well again.

They shook hands with the man, and left for the waterfront to the port, which was quite some distance away.

It would be a long walk carrying the two suitcases, which were quite heavy, but they eventually arrived at the harbour. Having missed one ferry, they had to wait several hours for another. Time was moving fast. Daniel, and especially Druscilla, were getting exhausted. There was a waiting room by the ferry, so they went in and sat to wait for the next boat. By this time, they were both very sleepy. Making sure that the suitcases were secure beneath their feet, they started to have small bouts of sleep. Suddenly, they were brought rudely from their slumber. A Soviet policeman shook Daniel's shoulder roughly and asked for his and his wife's identity. Daniel fumbled in his pockets, produced the identities, and gave them to the policeman.

He took a good look at them, and said, "Oh, you are a Russian. Where are you going?"

Daniel said, "To Istanbul. You see, we have just

been married, and we are going to spend our honeymoon there. That's why we have the suitcases with our clothes."

This seemed to satisfy the policeman's enquiries, and he left. Another sigh of relief came over them. They just hoped it would not be long before they boarded the ferry. Daniel and Druscilla did not have to wait long until a boat arrived from Istanbul. Meanwhile, they had purchased their fare and were eager to get on board. It was time to depart and, at last, they could relax, leaving the increasingly foreboding Soviet Union behind.

The crossing to Istanbul took twelve hours and, except for an understandable feeling of sadness in having to leave their homeland, it also meant that they were further away from Daniel's parents. It gave him a great deal of concern as to what might happen to them. His mind was abruptly taken away from thoughts of his parents when they arrived at Istanbul, as it was quite a shock to them. They were now in a Muslim country, and were very surprised by how modern and open it was. The streets were bustling, and the strange odours from spices and the coffee that people drank at the little cafes drowned their senses. This was totally unlike Russia, where everything appeared drab and, in many cases, depressing. However, they still had a problem— where to stay? The journey by ferry had been tedious, so it was essential to have a place to stay and get some rest. This was not going to be easy, not knowing the language. Besides, carrying their cases, they needed a place where they could leave them, and also try again to get a good night's rest. As the ferries went back and forth to Russia, Daniel thought that there must be people around who spoke Russian. He asked some people standing about near a bus stop if they spoke the language. Fortunately, one of them, a young man, did. He asked him if he knew of a reasonable place to stay. By this time, they were getting low on the money they had brought with them. Also, they had to find somewhere to change their roubles to lira. The young man who spoke to them in Russian said that, if they boarded the bus with him, he would show them where to get off. It was, apparently, not too far away. There, they would find small hotels or accommodation. Arriving at the place, the man announced that they had to leave the bus; they explained to the young man that they only had roubles to pay with. He said that he would pay for them, as it was only a short journey. As they left the bus, both Daniel and Druscilla thanked the man for his kindness, and Daniel shook his hand.

Although the street looked a little dingy, they took a good look around, and decided on a small place, thinking it would be cheaper. They knocked on the door, and a man opened it. He was wearing a red cap, which Daniel thought must be a fez. Daniel asked him if he could give them a place to sleep for the night. Replying in Russian— which came as a surprise to Daniel— the man said he could, and told them the price. He then enquired if they were married, asking if that was his wife, to which Daniel replied, "Yes, she is."

He asked where they had come from. Daniel said, "Russia."

The man added that he had also lived there, but had left many years ago. It was a good thing that the man spoke Russian; Daniel would have found him difficult to understand if he spoke Turkish. The host made them a meal— the first good meal they had eaten in days. Retiring to their room, they set about studying a map given to them by Daniel's father in case they were not sure of their route. They now had to determine how they would travel to Cyprus, and to take the quickest way to get there. They thought the train would cost too much money to reach the coast from Istanbul. Also, it was not convenient for attending to various functions; perhaps they could get lifts in vehicles going down the country. They had to decide quickly what to do, because, the next day they, would leave. The sooner they got to Cyprus, the better. Leaving his wife at the accommodation, Daniel went in search of a money-changer, as he now had no use for roubles. He would require Turkish lira, which he could also use in

Cyprus, where there was a large Turkish population. After a very agitated wait, his wife was pleased to see him back again. Druscilla asked how he had managed and if he had been able to change the roubles. Daniel told her he had changed all the money, and now had lira, but the money-changer had given him a very poor deal. Still, he had to do it. At least they would find it easier to settle any expenses. The next morning, they said goodbye to the man at the accommodation, and paid him what they owed.

*   *   *

Daniel said they should go back to the harbour, as he had seen a number of lorries there, and maybe they would be able to get a lift in one of them. This time, they caught a bus, as now they had the money to pay, so would not have to carry their suitcases walking there. The suitcases were their whole assets, and they had to make sure they were with them at all times. Arriving at the Ferry Port, Daniel made enquiries with some of the lorry drivers, and was surprised that a lot of them spoke Russian. Some of them were transporting goods from the docks to various parts of the country. Looking around and asking, they found a driver willing to give them a lift on condition he bought him a meal en route. It transpired that he was going as far as Adapozari. Daniel was pleased with this arrangement, as it would take them well on their way. At the town of Izmit, the vehicle stopped and visited a café where Daniel, as promised, bought him and themselves a meal. Feeling refreshed, back in the lorry, they made their way to Adapozari, which was the driver's destination. Thanking him for his kindness, and taking the suitcases, they stood for a while to look around. The lorry driver whose vehicle they had just left came across to them and pointed to another vehicle standing there. The driver said that he knew the other driver, and he was going to Ankara and would give them a lift. Daniel and Druscilla could not believe their luck, again saying goodbye to the driver, and again thanking him. They went over to the other vehicle, where the driver greeted them. They got into the lorry, which was much more comfortable than the last one, and started off for Ankara. The driver motioned to them to get into the truck. Back into the driver's seat, he set off for Ankara. To make the journey more interesting, talking in Russian, Daniel engaged the driver in conversation; he seemed interested to know where they were going and why. Daniel was able to tell him, in the few words the man could understand— he was not Russian by his appearance. Daniel said they had just been married and were going to Cyprus for a holiday. The driver was a little surprised when he heard this, saying it was very far to go for a holiday. It was a distance of about a hundred and fifty miles to Ankara. With the motion of the vehicle, Daniel and Druscilla felt sleepy, and were only awakened when the lorry stopped at a café or stopping places along the road for the driver to relieve himself, which gave the couple an opportunity to do the same. It gave them the chance to purchase some food and drink, too. They were feeling happy at their good fortune, that they had covered such a great distance at such a little cost and trouble. It was quite some time before they arrived in Ankara. The journey had been very tedious, and was beginning to become tiring. Getting out of the lorry, Daniel and Druscilla thanked the driver for the lift, and offered to give him something for his kindness, but he refused to take anything. It could be that he was rather taken with Druscilla's good looks. He took hold of her hand and kissed it, then, shaking hands with Daniel, walked away from them.

Druscilla, at this point, told Daniel that she did not feel too good. Perhaps it was the journey they had taken in the lorry that had made her feel unwell. Daniel looked at her and knew at once, being a doctor, that she was pregnant. He said they would find a hotel and stay the night there before leaving Ankara. Going outside the station, they found a small hotel, and booked themselves into it. Daniel carried both the suitcases, as he thought it too much for

Druscilla, as she did not feel well. That night, they had a good rest and some welcome food, both being exhausted after such a long journey. They very soon went to sleep. In the morning, Druscilla felt much better, and said she was fine. However, Daniel suggested that they stay another day and night to get rested for the next step of their journey. It would be a long way from Ankara to the next stop, a settlement called Adana. Fully rested, they checked out of the hotel and, with their cases, left for the railway station.

*   *   *

They caught a train to the next stop, Adana, which was approximately two hundred and fifty miles, and settled down for the journey. Daniel hoped that Druscilla would have no problems again, and would be able to travel, being so near to their goal. Besides, when they reached Cyprus, they would have more chance of coping with the present situation. It was fortunate that they had taken the train. If they had hitched another lift with a lorry, it would have been most uncomfortable for her, being three months pregnant. After arriving at Adana, which was the end of the line for them, the next place they had to get to, according to Daniel's map, was a place called Anumur, or another town called Alanya. They were unsure how they could reach these places. The train tickets had made a big hole in their finances; would they have enough money to get any further? They still had to get to Cyprus and Palestine. By this time, Druscilla said she was feeling much better, and would carry one of the cases again to give Daniel a rest. They were uncertain which place to make for: Anumur or Alanya. The first place was nearer, so they decided on it. If they had difficulty, they would try to get to Alanya. It was still some distance to travel to both places, and how could they get to them? Adana would be quite strange to them; it would not be like Ankara, which, to some degree, was more cosmopolitan. Daniel looked around the station and saw by the notices on the station signs that a train would be leaving for both the towns they wanted to reach. Although the notice was in Turkish, he could make out the names of the destinations. They were virtually down to their last lira. Would they have enough to pay for the journey? They both got on the train. To their surprise, it was not as costly as they had thought and, having purchased the tickets, they had a few lira left over. The train would take about two hours to get to Anumur, which would not be too long.

When they arrived at Anumur, they found that it was a small fishing village and, as Druscilla was feeling much better, they set off to the harbour, where they hoped that a fishing boat would take them to Cyprus. There were several boats there in the harbour. They approached a man whom they presumed to be a fisherman, and asked if he could take them to Cyprus. He replied that he could not do that, but he would introduce them to someone who, for a fee, might be able to do so. They walked with the man to a boat alongside the jetty, and he called to a person on the deck of one of the craft. Climbing onto the jetty, a man came up to them, and the fisherman explained to him what they wanted. The boat owner said it was not legal to take them to Cyprus. He then asked Daniel why he wanted to get there, saying it was not easy to smuggle anyone. Daniel said he had relatives there, and was spending a holiday with them. The fisherman, who spoke no Russian, could speak some English. He had often been into a Cyprus port. Daniel, who had a smattering of English, too, was able to understand him. They agreed to take them, but Daniel only had a small amount of lira left, and that was not enough for the journey. It seemed that they were going to be stuck here. Daniel asked the fisherman if he would take his wedding ring as payment, as well as the lira. Daniel then removed his wedding ring and gave it to the fisherman, telling him that it was eighteen carat gold, and would bring a good price. Daniel's wife took hold of his hand and, looking at her husband, tears came to her eyes. She said nothing, as she knew how desperate they were to get to Cyprus. Looking at the ring, the fisherman said he would not get very much for it; and asked if they had anything else they could give him. Daniel had a word with Druscilla, asking her to open the suitcase and see what they could barter. Opening it, she searched amongst the clothes, and brought out a silver pocket watch. It had been a present to Daniel from one of his uncles. It was one of the least valuable assets they had. They handed it to the fisherman, who seemed pleased with it and, putting it in his pocket, agreed to take them to Cyprus.

They then got on board the fishing boat with their cases and, full of trepidation, braced themselves for the sea journey, which would take a day and a night to complete. The fishing boat left the harbour, and Daniel hoped they would have a calm crossing to Cyprus, with Druscilla being pregnant. It worried him that she may not stand the voyage. Night was falling and, after a very uncomfortable sea crossing, they could see the outline of the Cypriot shore. The boat engines stopped and, with them stopping, the boat started wallowing in the sea, which made Druscilla feel sick. They were some distance from the land, and had to wait until it was dark before they could get ashore. As the night became darker, a small dinghy was lowered into the water, and the fishing boat extinguished its lights. Now it was very dark, and the owner of the boat indicated to Daniel and Druscilla to climb down to the dinghy. The oarsman pushed it away and started rowing for the shore; it seemed an eternity before they reached it. The man rowing the boat got out and started to pull it onto the beach whilst motioning them to get out. Picking up their two cases, and Druscilla regaining her composure, they climbed out onto the shore, which seemed to be in an isolated place. The oarsman shook hands with them quickly, and, pushing the boat into the water again, jumped on board and began to row away hurriedly.

All alone on the beach, panic began to strike them. What on earth would they do now? They could see lights a long distance away, but did not know how far it would be to walk. For a while, they felt hopeless, but decided to have a look around. In the dark, stumbling with their cases, with his wife feeling the effects of her pregnancy, they came to a road. This gave them hope, and Daniel thought perhaps they could be lucky if a vehicle came along. They both sat on the suitcases and waited, neither of them saying anything. After some time passed, out of the darkness, coming towards them were some lights. Their spirits soared, and they thought this could be a lorry or some other kind of vehicle that would take them to the lights, which was a town or village. As the vehicle approached, they waved their arms. It was a lorry, but it did not stop. Daniel and Druscilla were devastated; they had visions of spending the night alone on the roadside. The lorry, after it had passed them, suddenly stopped, and then started reversing back to them. A man got out who, by his speech, was a Greek. Daniel tried to converse with him in Russian, but he just shook his head. He motioned them to put their cases in the back of the small truck. They then got in with the driver. Again, Daniel tried to make conversation with him, but to no avail. It was obvious that they would have to use a different tactic. The man turned to them again, smiling. Pointing to the lights, he kept saying, "Yes, yes."

Believing that he was trying to tell them he was going to the town, Daniel smiled back at him and nodded in agreement, at the same time putting his hands to his head and mouth, indicating that they needed some food and sleep.

Arriving at the town, whose name they did not even know, was to cause yet another problem. As they had no money, where would they stay? It seemed pointless to ask the lorry driver anything with the language problem, so they shook hands with him and acknowledged his kindness. They then started looking around. They seemed to be in the centre of the small town. It was beginning to get light. Noticing some shops were open and having not had any food or drink for some time, they were very hungry. The fishermen had given then a drink of coffee when on the boat, at least. How could they buy anything without

16

money? Also, they must have accommodation, especially in view of his wife's condition. Daniel spotted a taverna that appeared to be open. They went inside to see if they could beg or, with some of their valuables, make an exchange, not only having to eat; they had to find some place to stay. They were very tired and weary after the journey from Adana, but luck was again on their side. The owner was Jewish, and very liberal with his hospitality. Daniel, speaking in Russian, asked him if it was possible to give his wife and himself some food. At first, the man did not understand him, and shook his head. Daniel then pointed to his mouth to indicate that they wanted something to eat. Thinking that the man might be Jewish, Daniel began to speak in Hebrew. The man then recognised him as Jewish, like himself. At that, he told them to sit, and immediately set about getting some food for them. The man then asked them where they had come from, and Daniel related the story of their journey thus far. Whilst enjoying the food that the host had provided, Daniel discussed other matters with him; why they had left Russia, and the circumstances that had led them to make the decision. After the meal, the man asked them if they had a place to stay. Daniel said 'no'. He said he was going to ask him if he knew of somewhere. The man said he could help him in this matter. He had a friend whom he knew would give them accommodation. He then gave them the address, and told them where to find him. With what was happening to them, it gave Daniel and Druscilla a good feeling. As they were ready to leave the taverna, they told the main they had no money, and asked if he would take something in exchange.

"No, no," he replied.

He said that it was a pleasure to meet another Jewish person, and he was glad to help them. He then said his friend would look after them well. Daniel shook hands with his host and thanked him for his hospitality, saying he hoped he would see him again. Then they left with their cases to find the friend's house.

* * *

From the directions the man at the taverna had given them, they found the house; it was quite neat, located in its own grounds and approached by a pathway from a walled doorway. It seemed that a blessing had been bestowed on them after a difficult journey. They had just knocked at the door of the house when they were greeted by a man in his fifties, clean-shaven and wearing a brightly coloured shirt. They told him who they were, and who had sent them. Inviting them in, he introduced his wife whilst motioning them to sit. It turned out, during the conversation they had, that the man was Armenian, and his wife was Jewish. The family had come to Cyprus many years ago from Salonika to start a new life; indeed, he had been born here. His father had kept a shoe shop and also sold clothing, which, in time, had made them wealthy. His parents were now dead, and he owned the business. After a pause, the Armenian asked them if they would like something to drink.

"Yes," responded Daniel.

Refreshments were brought to them by the Armenian's wife. The conversation then turned to Daniel and Druscilla. The Armenian asked why they had left Russia. The doctor told him the whole story. Arriving here in the town, his friend at the taverna had told them that he would accommodate them temporarily. Andropoulous, as the man was called, said he was pleased to have them. Then, looking at the doctor's wife, he said he could see why they needed a place to stay as a matter of urgency.

After all they had suffered, a night's rest was wonderful, and it was a luxury to sleep in a good bed in pleasant surroundings. The next morning, at breakfast, the doctor mentioned to Andropoulous that he had no money, but had a few valuable possessions in the way of jewellery and heirlooms. These, he was reluctant to part with, as they were better value than money, which always had to be changed to different currencies. Also, he could use them to bargain with. Daniel's wife became poorly again, and was not in a fit state to travel. She was having difficulty in carrying a child, which was now beginning to show. While they were in the house, the Armenian said he had to leave for his shop, but his wife would tend to their needs. When the man's wife was out of hearing in another part of the house, the doctor said to Druscilla, "I'm afraid we will have to stay here for a while. I will look for some work and, with the money, see if we can rent an apartment."

That evening, when the host returned home, Daniel mentioned to him what he intended to do, regarding finding a job. The man thought it was the sensible course to take, especially due to his wife's condition. He also said he would help them to find work. Knowing they required help at the local clinic, he would make some enquiries for him. Nothing happened for a few days, but, when the man arrived home from his shop one evening, he said he had some good news for Daniel. He was required to attend an interview at the clinic the next day. Of course, he was delighted to hear such news, and thanked Andropoulous for making the enquiries for him. The next day, bidding his wife goodbye with a smile, and kissing her, he set off to the clinic for the interview. Arriving there, he was shown into an ante-room, and waited. A large man with dark skin soon appeared in a while coat. Daniel took him to be Arabic, but, in fact, he was Turkish. He greeted Daniel with a handshake, and then sat. He questioned him about his qualifications as a doctor and what experience he had. Daniel, who had brought his papers with him, showed them to him. Looking them over, he seemed to acknowledge them. He then asked him why he had left Russia. Daniel told him that he had worked at a town clinic, but had to leave his job because there was not enough money to support him, and, being the youngest, he had to leave. He had heard that there were better opportunities abroad, and had decided to come to Cyprus for a better life, and the weather was also more amenable. Daniel did not want him to know the real reason, obviously. After he had answered a few medical questions, the Turk was satisfied by his answers, saying that he would employ him temporarily, but, if he proved he was capable, it could become permanent, and he could start his work the next day. Daniel then shook hands with the Turk and, full of optimism, hummed his way back to the house to tell his wife the good news. This made her feel better; now she felt more secure. On the assumption he now had work, he would look for an apartment to rent, as the clinic would be paying him a salary. Searching around for a few days, he was in luck. He had found a flat that was not too far away from the clinic, and it was ready to move in to. Daniel told his Armenian friend of his good fortune. The next day, he told him that he would now leave them and move to the flat, as Daniel did not want to burden his host anymore. Thanking the man for his generosity and his kindness for having him and his wife, he took what possessions he had, including the two suitcases. He said goodbye to the Armenian and his wife, telling them he would keep in touch with them. Then, with Druscilla, he proceeded to find the apartment.

* * *

Arriving there gave them a sense of security. They had been virtually homeless for what seemed a long time, but could now settle down and get on with their lives. The flat was partly furnished, but, at the moment, was adequate for their requirements. They now knew they were in a town called Morphou on the north side of the island, which was fairly isolated. They had to stay here until the baby was born. Everything seemed to be going right for them, and they felt more relaxed. Although things were going well for them, Daniel was still worried about what might happen to his parents. He had tried many times sending letters, but never got any replies, but one day, he did. It was a miracle that it found him, much to his delight, and albeit it being several weeks old. In it, his father had said they were well,

20

and life in Russia was as normal as it could be. He had not been troubled up to the present. As he had said before, maybe it was because he was a doctor. It pleased Daniel to hear this news, and he was relieved to know that his parents were all right.

His wife was now due to have the baby. From his professional prognosis, he assured her that he thought she would not have any problems, and, as he worked at the clinic, she would be well looked after. Druscilla was now twenty-three years old, and Daniel was twenty-eight. Although they knew that a child would not be easy to deal with if they wanted to reach Palestine, they were happy at the prospect of having the baby, and Daniel hoped they would have a boy.

It was now six months since they had left Russia. It would soon be Christmas. They both felt a little sad, as Daniel always had his family around them at this time of the year, but that was to be put to one side, as his wife was going into labour. He quickly rushed her to the clinic. The next day, she gave birth to a healthy boy. It was the twenty-forth of December. They were overjoyed with the outcome. The child would keep them busy and take their minds off their ultimate goal; for a time, at least. After a few days, Druscilla left the clinic and returned to the flat. Now, they had to decide a name for their son. Daniel suggested that he could be called Aaron, after his father, but Druscilla said she thought that sounded too Jewish, and that Arun sounded better. Daniel agreed with her, so they settled for the name.

*   *   *

As time passed, it was obvious that they would not be able to travel with the baby to Palestine. News coming out of Europe was very disturbing, with the rise of the Nazis and their leader, Hitler. Reports reaching them were horrendous. Hearing how the Jewish population was being treated upset them and made them feel more insecure. They

21

had no option now but to stay in Cyprus for the time being. Daniel said they still had insufficient money saved to buy a place in Palestine, even if they sold the valuables. They felt safer here in Cyprus, as the British had an influence here. They made the decision to stay until the boy was six months old, then he would be able to stand the journey when they decided to leave.

Daniel was a very good doctor. He was popular with his patients, and had made many friends in the Greek and Turkish population. He was humbled by their kindness and generosity to him. As time went on, they were settled for the time being, and their life was quite good, but they were still very worried about what was happening in Europe, with all the bad news. They were concerned that it may even reach Cyprus if there was to be a war. It was now May, and they were beginning to get agitated thinking of how to organise their departure for Palestine. They still felt trapped, stuck, as they were in the small town of Morphou; it was not a place from which one could get a boat to Palestine. They had to get to Limassol or Larnaca if they had any chance of succeeding in their goal. Deciding they would soon have to make the effort to leave, they gathered together what they would require for themselves and the child, and packed the two suitcases they had brought with them originally. Now, they had to make up their minds how they would leave without causing any problems or suspicion. Daniel said he would tell the clinic that they would take a short holiday and visit Limassol, but would give the clinic time to find a substitute whilst he was away. They had kept up their friendship with the Armenian and his wife, whom they trusted. They told him of their plans. He was very sad to hear they were going, and agreed to keep things confidential, for their sake. Also, he would organise their departure, as he had lived there all his life and knew of someone who would take them to Limassol and on the day they would leave; he would arrange the transport for them.

* * *

The day to move on arrived and, late that evening, they left the flat. Daniel had given the Armenian the rent he owed to pay the landlord, who said he would do that for them. Waiting outside for them was a vehicle that would take them to Limassol. They arrived there in the evening, and Daniel found it very different to Morphou. He saw numbers of mosques, churches and Greek and Turkish shops. Everyone seemed to be mixing amicably with each other. Their next move was to pay the driver. Now that they had money to spare, it was necessary for them to find a place to stay, and they eventually found a place; a small lodging house in one of the side streets that was quite reasonable in price. The woman of the house, who Daniel thought must be the owner, welcomed them inside. She appeared to be in her fifties and, perhaps, a little overweight. Nevertheless, she was of a jovial nature. She was a little surprised that they had a baby, but, by her expression, she looked quite pleased, and at once offered to hold the child while Daniel and Druscilla were shown to a room. Again, it was good to know that they had made great strides to reach their destination of Palestine. Daniel rose early the next morning, and told Druscilla that he was going to the harbour to see what the situation was, and to try to get a boat to Palestine. When he got there, quite a number of people were on the quayside. He stopped and asked a person if any of the ferries or boats sailed to Palestine. The man did not understand what Daniel had said. He then touched a man's shoulder near to him. The man asked Daniel what he wanted, talking to him in Greek, which was a language he now understood— working at the clinic, he had soon picked it up. The man ushered him to a small group of people standing there. He thanked the man, who then walked away. Daniel asked the group, in Greek, what they were waiting for. Shaking their heads, they spoke in Russian, which was a surprise to him. He had not heard Russian spoken since they had left Turkey. This cheered

Daniel up. He then asked them why they were waiting. They said they had been there for a week, waiting for a boat that would take them to Palestine, but did not know when one would arrive. They said that they did not know which port it would go to there. It transpired that the group were Jewish refugees, and had come in small parties from different areas around Romania and the Black Sea area. They, too, were aware of what was happening in Russia to the Jewish population and, like Daniel, had made the effort and accepted the hardship to pursue their aim, which was Palestine.

*　　*　　*

Early the next day, Daniel went to the harbour and, on the quayside, the little group was still there; they seemed not to have moved from where they had been the previous day. Their clothes were ragged. They also looked pale and thin. How they would survive a journey to Palestine, Heaven only knew. Apparently, they had a few pieces of clothing to keep them covered when they slept on the floor near a building, which gave them some shelter. Daniel was very upset to see his fellow men, women and small children in such a poor condition; he only hoped they would be successful in reaching Palestine. He counted himself and Druscilla as being fortunate having good food and a bed to enjoy. The British, who had an influence over Cyprus, seemed to take very little notice of the people who were gathered on the quay. There were a few soldiers, and also several other officials, who Daniel thought might be Cypriot policemen. Daniel thought this could be the opportunity they were waiting for, but how was he to know when the boat was to arrive? The thought of missing the boat to Palestine was causing him a good deal of anxiety. Daniel went back to his lodging house and, full of excitement and hope, explained to his wife what he had found out. They now had to make a decision for their next move, and how to leave with the child. Daniel said he would periodically go down to the quay to see if a boat had come in.

After doing this for a day and a night, he found it very stressful, but was determined that he would not miss an opportunity to leave Cyprus. He did this for four nights and, on the fifth day, as he did his periodic walk to the harbour, he was surprised to see a quite a big vessel coming in. He immediately tried to find out where it was going and when it would leave. He waited for a while. The boat was too big to come close in. However, a small boat left the harbour for the bigger ship. He saw they were taking passengers and goods from it. When the passengers eventually landed, they seemed to be a very mixed lot. He stopped one of them and asked in Greek where they had come from. He replied, "From Beirut."

Questioning him further, Daniel, to his delight and joy, discovered that the next port of call would be Haifa, then to Beirut, and back to Limassol. What he now wanted to know was when the boat would leave again. He picked out a person who he thought looked like a crew member, as he was in a kind of uniform. The boat was Greek owned, so, hopefully, Daniel could converse with him in Greek— this was so. The man said it was in the harbour for two days to unload goods, then to take on any passengers. It would then leave for Haifa. Daniel hurried back to his wife to tell her what he knew. Now they had to make their minds up when to leave. They discussed the situation with the woman of the house, who understood their plight and was very sympathetic towards them. She had made good friends with them, especially with his wife and the baby. She said that she had never had any children of her own, and it was, to her, a pleasure to hold and nurse the child. It was agreed that they would leave the next morning, and they hoped that they would be able to board the ship. If they failed to get on, the woman said they were welcome to return to her house, but, at the same time, she hoped they would be successful. The next day, with all their possessions in the two suitcases, which, by now, were getting a little worse for wear, they said goodbye to the woman, thanking her for her kindness, and set off for the harbour. They then joined with the people who were waiting. No passengers had yet been taken on board; they seemed to be loading various goods onto the tender, also taking on animals, either sheep or goats, in crates. Even two coffins were put on the tender. Daniel shuddered, and hoped this was not a bad omen. At a small kiosk, a man was selling tickets, and Daniel wondered how much it was going to cost. When his turn came to purchase the tickets for himself and his wife, he found that there were several means of travel. You could have a cabin, which was expensive. Then there were hammocks under a shelter deck, or you could stay on the rear part of the boat with no facilities. They had to decide quickly. With a baby, they must have decent accommodation. Daniel asked for a cabin, even though it was to take a lot of his remaining money. Eventually, the passengers were taken on board the boat. Daniel did not see if the poor Romanian group had managed to get on. Struggling with their suitcases and the child, they eventually got on board. The cabin they had was very small, but it was better than sleeping on the deck. Besides, they were in a much more optimistic mood. They were now in sight of their goal. It made them much happier, so a little discomfort was not a problem to them, after all, they had got used to it with the recent journeys they had taken.

CHAPTER II
The Arrival and Settlement

After an overnight journey to Haifa, the family were relieved that their arrival would be an end to the trauma and discomfort they had been through, especially with their child, now nearly three years old. They had always hung on tenaciously to the two battered suitcases, which were the only possessions they had, and had even managed to keep in their possession the few valuables they believed would enable them to begin a new life. They disembarked from the ferry and, setting foot onto their Promised Land, became quite emotional, and tears appeared in their eyes. All around them were shouts and crying as the Jewish passengers, some in a very pitiful state, their clothes dirty and worn, prostrated themselves on the ground, ignoring everything around them. When the Aserov family finally realised that they were now safely ashore, they began to see how different everything was, not like the quiet rural area that had been their home in Russia. It was quite a culture shock for them all. They had never travelled out of Russia before now. All around were Arabs or Palestinians in their flowing robes and their particular headwear. There were also a number of British police and Palestinian police. Of course, he remembered that the British had a mandate over Palestine and virtually ruled it.

People began to disperse, but not all of them; only those who carried a permit were allowed to go. The rest were taken to a building in the harbour front to be interrogated. The Aserovs, being in that category, waited their turn, but were not unduly worried, except for the child. They had to find somewhere to stay quickly, and hoped there would not be any problem with coming here. Their turn came for the interview, and they were questioned by the police. They asked him his name, and if it was his wife and child, and why he had come to Palestine. His answers were very much the same as all the previous people who had been interviewed. This seemed not to bother the policeman very much. He then asked him his profession. Daniel replied, saying he was a qualified doctor, and he had his papers with him to prove it. These, he had taken with him when he had left. His father thought it may help him; also, he had the map his father had given him. When the policeman had seen his papers and questioned him more, he was taken to one side and told to wait. Daniel now became very frightened, and his wife was the same. What could be wrong? About ten minutes or so later, the policeman came back with a man in a British army uniform, and he then introduced him to Daniel. He seemed very friendly, and the officer said to him, "I believe you are a doctor."

Daniel replied, "Yes."

The officer then asked him about his life in Russia and what he specialised in. Daniel said he was a General Practitioner, but had also had experience with surgery, as his father was a doctor, too and he had assisted him, at times. The officer then asked him if he would like to take a post at the local military hospital, which also cared for nationalities such as Palestinians, Jordanians, Lebanese, and other foreign nationals.

Daniel glanced at his wife, who was standing some distance away holding the child and keeping watch on the suitcases, whilst also feeling very worried as to what was going on between her husband and the officer. Although they had had a very rough and uncomfortable journey, their appearance was quite presentable. This may have been the reason he was picked out. As the officer moved away, Daniel came over to his wife with a smile on his face and, looking very pleased, he told her what the officer had said. He would take them to the hospital right away, where they would find him accommodation.

They travelled in the officer's vehicle through the crowded streets, with the numerous shops and bazaars. Everything seemed so busy, with many different nationalities among them. He did notice some Jews, distinct in their broad-rimmed hats, with beards and side locks. It was difficult to take everything in, as events had moved so quickly. Soon, they came to a white stone building on one level in a garden-like surrounding, with a number of small buildings around it. They were greeted at the hospital by a man in a white coat, and the officer introduced him as the head of the hospital. He was Arab by his looks, and was quite formal, but polite. The officer left, bidding them a friendly goodbye.

*   *   *

Daniel and his wife, with the child, followed the man into the hospital. They sat in a room, and he said, "Perhaps, before we talk about things, you would like to have some food."

Daniel looked at his wife, and said it would please them very much, as they had had little to eat in the last twenty-four hours. At that, the doctor rang a bell, and a Palestinian or person of Arabic origin appeared. He was told to bring some food and drink. In the meantime, the man said they would be given accommodation in one of the hospital buildings. The servant came with the food and drink, and he left. The man in the white coat also left, and said he would return later. Daniel and Druscilla were very happy, and could hardly believe what had happened to them. He thought about how happy his father would be to know how it had all turned out for him, and, at the same time, what was happening to his parents in Russia was on his mind. Having eaten, and his wife taking care of the child, the man returned, took them to their quarters, and

29

told them to make themselves at home, saying he would speak to Daniel the next day.

In the morning of the next day, the head of the hospital, Mr. Ahmood, who appeared to be of Arabic origin, introduced Daniel to other members, and told him what his duties would be, together with the wages he would have. After he had finished with his introductions, Daniel was quite confident that he could do the work, as it was not dissimilar to what he had already experienced. He commenced his work the next day, and settled down with considerable enthusiasm and, knowing that he was at least, at the moment, quite secure, life suddenly took on a better feeling.

*   *   *

The days went by, and Daniel did his work in a professional way, and was quite liked by the patients he attended. Druscilla, too, was happy, and the boy was growing fast. They had now been in Palestine for nearly six months. Daniel was quite happy, and day-to-day things seemed to be going along quite well, but, on the outside of the hospital, news was coming in of the trouble in Germany, where a man called Hitler was making trouble. The country was in a poor economic state, and he was putting the blame on the Jewish population. Since 1935, trouble had been brewing. People were frightened; mostly Jews or people who were related to them by marriage. Some Jews who were wealthy or who had successful businesses decided to flee the country before things got worse, and many emigrated to America, where there were others who had managed to flee from Russia and other European states. It seemed reasonably quiet in Palestine, although there were instances of rebellion amongst some Palestinians who wanted the British out, and also a number of Jewish dissidents and other groups who were calling for a state in the name of Israel. The British were trying to keep some of these groups controlled, which was difficult.

Both Arabs and Jews hated the British occupiers. Inevitably, there were casualties, and some ended up in the hospital where Daniel worked.

These uprisings were not too serious to begin with, but, as things deteriorated in Europe, more refugees were arriving with stories of what was happening in Germany and Russia. It seemed that the world had gone mad and nobody could know what would happen next. There were quiet periods in Palestine, and most people went about their business as usual. Even Christmas seemed to bring some peace and stability to the 'Holy Land'. Time was forging ahead. Daniel had now been working in the hospital for nearly eighteen months. Palestine was now being plagued with fighting between Arabs and Jews. The year was 1939, and things were going from bad to worse in Europe. There was a fear that war may break out, as Hitler's army was bent on expansion of the 'German state', and was building tension in Europe. The British were still in Palestine and Iraq, and had military bases there. The French, too, were in Syria and the Lebanon, with military forces, as well. It was a worrying time, as the news coming out of Europe was very disturbing and the stories of horror and persecution were unbelievable. Daniel wondered what might happen. Would he be safe even here now? Perhaps America would have been the safest place, as nothing was heard from there of any troubles. After a very tense period, more news came through of what was happening, and then, in September 1939, the news came that Hitler had invaded Poland. This, of course, activated the British, and they declared war on Germany because of the German invasion of Poland. Things took a change in Palestine. The British had increased their troop numbers in the Middle East, and a naval force was operating in the Mediterranean. Things were also changing for Daniel. What if the war spread to the Mediterranean? Would he be safe with his family in Haifa, where there had been clashes between Jews and Palestinians? He discussed this with his wife, and thought it might be a good idea to find a place somewhere outside the

31

town, in the country somewhere. Although being Jewish, the family had rarely visited a synagogue. Religion was forbidden in Russia, and they did their rituals privately at home. So it would not be too difficult to move away and remain near enough to his work. Having been paid for his work, he was in a position to buy a house somewhere. He also still had the few valuable pieces that he had managed to keep, which, perhaps, he could barter with. Daniel had come across some Jewish people who had bought property from Arabs, these mostly being shop premises. It might be possible to buy a house somewhere in the country. He was used to a rural life in Russia, and could get away from the noise and smells of the streets. Talking, one day, to a Jewish friend, he brought this subject up, and his friend said he knew where he could enquire. One day, he decided he would make an enquiry, so he took his friend's directions and ended up in a narrow, dingy street with an Arabic sign above the door of a more dingy house. He knocked at the door, and a young man came. Daniel introduced himself, and said he was looking for a house for his family; himself, his wife, and small son. The man asked Daniel what area he wanted to live in. Daniel said he did not know the surrounding areas, but, as long as it was not too far from the hospital, it will be suitable. The main said he knew of a place that the owner, a Palestinian, wanted to sell, as he was moving to Jordan, where his wife came from. He would not be isolated there, as one or two Jewish families had bought houses there. This sounded ideal to Daniel, and he said he would like to see the place before he made an offer on it. They both agreed to go next day to view it.

* * *

The next day, he took a little time off from his work, and set off in the man's very rickety, old car, out to about ten kilometres in the country. Driving over very rough roads, they went up a hill and stopped at a whitewashed stone house. Daniel and the man got out and, immediately, Daniel was impressed by the view of the green area that surrounded it. The man pointed out the houses that he said were owned by the Jewish families, which were some distance away. These looked to be new, but the man said they were the original houses that had been modernised. The house for sale stood in four hectares of land, and had olive trees and a vegetable plot. Further down the hill was another house, smaller, but it had a big cypress tree near it, and he could also see that some animals were there: goats, a donkey and a number of sheep. The doctor did not have a vehicle, but he did not think it would be too difficult to cycle until he was able to buy a car. As they approached the house, the Palestinian owner came to the door, and the man talked to him in Arabic. Although Daniel had learnt quite a lot of Arabic, the men talked so fast, at the same time throwing their arms about. They were discussing the price. After a lot more gesticulating, they shook hands and the man came back to Daniel and told him what the man wanted; he had told him he wanted too much. The man said, "But I told him what you would pay, and he finally agreed."

They left the hillside and went back to the hospital. Daniel thanked the Arab, and said he would meet him again after he had discussed the house with his wife.

A few days passed, and Daniel had saved some money from his wages. He also sold two pieces of gold and a diamond bracelet, but it was not enough for the purchase. Daniel was beginning to get a little disappointed with not being able to raise the money. He thought that his friend could maybe help him with a loan. He met his friend and asked him. His friend said he did not have that much money available, but suggested that perhaps the local rabbi might help him. Daniel took this advice and approached the rabbi. Having never seen Daniel at the synagogue, he was a little cautious, but, when Daniel explained that his work at the hospital meant it was crucial for him to be there, but he did observe the faith and always practised it at home, the rabbi warmed to Daniel and said he understood that his work was a priority. Daniel then explained his financial situation to him, and the rabbi agreed to loan him the balance of the monies, but with a condition that he would like to see him now and again in the synagogue with his family. Having settled the deal, it was now time to see the Arab agent and make a purchase for the house on the hill. Daniel had told his wife that the house would be ideal for them, and the boy would be able to play and breathe fresh air among the olive trees. It also needed some work to modernise it, he explained, to look like the other Jewish houses that were there.

* * *

Events were unfolding very fast in the world; fear was spreading all over Europe, and the news was getting worse, in that the war was spreading to other countries. It was rumoured that Russia would take up arms with the Germans. This made Daniel and his family more depressed, as he had no idea what was happening to his parents back in Russia. There was a lot of activity going on around him. He was still at the military hospital and was experiencing some of the problems that were happening to the population. There were clashes between Arab and Jewish groups. The British were getting considerable aggravation from both groups, but, as the war had begun, it was obvious that the British would stay. Palestine was a vital strategic outpost for them. Also, they had air and military bases in Iraq and their allies, the French, were linked with them in the Lebanon and Syria, and also in North Africa, with the British in the Sudan and Egypt. To make things worse, it was rumoured that the Italians were allying with the Germans. This was really worrying, as the fighting was getting closer. The British had now started to build up a powerful naval force, based in Malta and Alexandria. He knew that some naval ships were in that area, as they called Haifa to take on oil fuel.

Daniel told his wife that he would leave his quarters at the hospital and move out to the countryside to the house, of which he now had ownership. The Palestinian had handed him the titles to his house and land, and was now eager to move. At the end of the month, he informed the hospital that he was leaving his quarters, and told them he was moving to the country, about ten kilometres out of town. The military had now increased in numbers, and could fill any gaps in ther medical trades.

* * *

The day came when the family finally packed everything, not forgetting the two battered cases that had been a life-saver to them in times of need. The boy was doing well and, after all the discomfort and trauma they had suffered, they had much to be grateful for. Arun was now nearly three years old, and would grow up in a much more pleasant area than the busy and dusty town. They knew now that moving would be a strain for them for a while. The day came for them to move with their few possessions. The doctor and wife had been well thought of, and he was looked upon as a kind and compassionate man. An orderly, who had driven him, at times, for hospital duties, said he would take them, but it would have to be when he was not required for duty. They waited in anticipation for him to come. Soon, the orderly appeared, and they got into the vehicle and drove to the house. Druscilla had not seen the place before and at first sight remarked how green and pleasant it was, with the olive trees and a vine growing up the side of the house. They got out of the vehicle and Daniel thanked the driver, shook his hand, and hoped that, one day, they would meet again.

The family entered the house and immediately began to organise the rooms. They did not have any furniture or food, except they saw a small table and two chairs. Also, in one of the bedrooms, were two low beds, left by the previous owner, who had not wanted to take them to Jordan. Also, he had left the blankets with a note in Arabic saying he hoped they would enjoy the house and had left the blankets as a gift. It pleased them immensely to know the man had considered them. The one thing that they needed was food. Along the bottom of the hill there were one or two houses in a row. He had noticed, when passing, that a stall outside one of the houses was displaying different fruits. Daniel said to his wife he would go down the hill and see if he could buy something for them to eat. She agreed, and off he went down the dusty road that served the house. There was a stall at the bottom, and he bought some melons and vegetables. The shop owner, an Arab, also had some lentils and flour, some of which Daniel bought. Fortunately, he had enough money, as the hospital paid what was owing to him. Feeling quite elated, he set off back up the hill with his purchases. His wife was delighted that at least they would eat. In the house was a small electric stove, and each room was lighted by a single electric lamp. They were glad to have these facilities. Daniel had seen them when he viewed the house. Being quite an old house, he assumed that the electricity must have been connected when the Jewish houses further up the hill were modernised. After eating, they said prayers, and thanked God for their survival and for the fortunate things that had happened to them. After a fitful night's sleep, they woke up to a bright sunny day, and could hear the sound of goats bleating. Stepping outside the house, Daniel could see a little gathering of houses nearly at the foot of the hill. They were spaced a distance apart, the nearest one to them looking very well kept and pretty, with a large cedar tree nearby. Around it was land that was being grazed by some sheep and goats. A number of olive trees were also scattered about. He went inside and told his wife he would help her tidy up the house, but she said she would do that, and asked if he could take the boy for a walk, to which he agreed.

As he walked down the hill with the boy, a man approached him and introduced himself as his neighbour further above him. He said he had come to Palestine ten years ago from Russia. This made Daniel listen to him more intently. Daniel told him how and when he and his wife had arrived, and that he was a qualified doctor. This seemed to make the man more attentive, and he invited the doctor to visit them when he had time. At that, they both said 'shalom' and went their separate ways. Daniel was in a very happy mood, and thought about how lucky he was to be in the situation he was in, but there was something that was worrying him. He had to find work soon; otherwise, he would not be able to survive or pay back his liabilities. On his return to the house, he discussed the situation with Druscilla, and decided that, the next day, he would go to the town to enquire if he could find a post. He did not have the experience of any work other than as a doctor, and now, not being able to return to the military hospital with the war, it was obvious the British would have more manpower at their disposal. He had heard there was a small Jewish clinic in the town sited near the synagogue. Although he had not been in the synagogue, he had talked with the rabbi. So, to get to town, he went to the bottom of the hill— the area he understood was part of Mount Carmel. He had, occasionally, seen buses passing, so he made enquiries at the shop that was at the bottom. The Arab owner said buses did go into town, mainly early in the morning, to take children to school, and did not arrive back until late afternoon. He enquired if it took any passengers, to which the Arab replied, "It all depends if there is room, and if the driver is in a good mood."

He explained to his wife what the shopkeeper had said, and got up early the next day to wait for the bus. It came, and stopped near the shop. A number of children also appeared. The driver got out, went into the shop, and came out carrying something he had just bought: a packet of cigarettes. Daniel asked the driver if he could get on the bus to town. The Arab looked hard at him and asked in Arabic why he wanted to go to the town. Daniel replied in Arabic, at which he was becoming very good by now. He told the

Arab he was a doctor and was going to the clinic to try to get a position there. The driver agreed to let him get on the bus, and he then drove into town. The bus fare was only a few shekels.

Arriving in town, he made his way to the clinic and made himself known to an orderly, saying he would like to see the head doctor, or whoever was in charge. A man appeared, who was rather large, but had a hint of a smile upon his face. Daniel explained to him how he had arrived there and what he had previously been doing. This made the man more inquisitive, and he asked many more questions, especially why he worked for the military hospital, as the British were not very popular. Daniel said that he really had no option; he was more or less ordered by the military. Besides, with all the stress and uncertainty he had been through with his family, it had been a godsend to him, at the time. The man motioned to Daniel to follow him. They both went into a small office where they discussed further questions. Daniel was feeling quite nervous and, with all the questioning, was wondering what would happen next. The man said that he was a refugee, and had arrived from Germany some ten years previously. He knew professional people had suffered, and he was fortunate to get away before the situation got worse, but many of his friends, and even some of his family, had been arrested and imprisoned. The man finally said they could find a post for him, for which Daniel thanked him, very pleased and relieved. It seemed, from what the doctor had told him, that most of the refugees who had arrived before the war had started were not professionals, but mainly poor peasants. He warned Daniel that the situation was going to get worse. Already, news had come in that the Italians had sided with Germany and had now invaded Tripolitania— Libya. The hospital was now also dealing with casualties caused by opposition groups, both Jewish and Palestinian. The British had imposed a curfew, and people could be shot or arrested if they did not obey. Things were beginning to look a lot less 'rosy', and life had to be taken more seriously.

Daniel managed to find the bus in time to return home. On arriving home, he was delighted to tell his wife about his conversation with the doctor at the clinic, and added that she would be pleased to know he had been given a position there. Now he would have to find a means of transport, because he thought that the bus was not going to be reliable enough. He was able to convince the bus driver that he now had a job at the clinic, and asked him if he could take him until he got a vehicle of his own. The Arab driver was a little impressed with Daniel, because Arabs or Jews and most nationalities respected doctors who were, by nature, life savers, not life takers. Besides, he may need him one day.

*   *   *

Everything was going well for the family. The house had been improved, and looked quite tidy and orderly. The boy was growing, and they would soon have to find a suitable school for his education. Daniel had noticed vehicles coming and going from outside his neighbour's house. The man had told him when they met that he would be very welcome to visit them. Daniel thought that this might be an opportune time to pay him a visit. The family made itself as presentable as it could, and left the house to walk up the hill to the neighbour. The man of the house welcomed them, and introduced them to his family, of which there seemed to be quite a number. There were about six or eight people in the room; the man's elderly parents, two sons in their twenties, and two girls of school age. After a while, the men asked the sons to bring the family some food and drink. Daniel had told the neighbour that he was a doctor, adding that he had been given a position at the clinic in town. His only problem was transport. One of the men said they went to town every day, as they worked there. One of them was working for a clothing company; the other owned a shop selling provisions. They both had enough money to own cars, and the one son who kept the shop also took his sisters to a Jewish school in the town. The son who worked for the clothing company said he would be pleased to take him into town and bring him back again until he was able to get a car. In Russia, Daniel had never had the means to own a vehicle; both he and his father always had to use public transport or, locally, *troikas*. He did not know how to drive.

Everything was arranged between them and, the next day, he was picked up by the son, and they drove into town. At an agreed time, he would bring the doctor back home in the evening before the curfew was in place. Daniel had been so busy trying to organise his life that he had, for a moment, forgotten what was happening around him and his family. The European war was getting more intense. A trickle of refugees was coming into Palestine. These dispossessed were mainly from North Africa and Egypt where, in Alexandria, there was quite a large Jewish population. They were now leaving, as the Italians, having invaded Libya, were moving towards Egypt, so it was easier to go overland to Palestine. At least, for the time being, they would be safe. British forces were building in many areas, including Iraq, Palestine and Egypt. The war was spreading rapidly over large areas of Europe. Daniel thought everything and everybody had gone mad. Had he left one potential Hell and found himself in another? It was still uncertain what would happen if Palestine was invaded. Everyone was worried about being invaded. They did have a degree of hope, knowing the British would hold Palestine tenaciously, by reason of a vital necessity: oil. The main pipeline terminated at Haifa and started in Iraq, and this would be well protected by the British Forces stationed there. Also, the coastal area of Palestine would have the security of the large naval force stationed in Alexandria, Malta and Gibraltar, but the greatest factor in the equation was that Turkey had declared herself neutral, and this meant that the Lebanon, Syria and Palestine had a barrier between Europe and them, and it would be difficult for the

Axis powers to access Palestine by an overland route. Although the war gave him concern and made life more difficult, he knew that, to survive, he had to get on with his family's life together. That was the whole reason for coming from Russia, where life for the Jews was becoming intolerable, and the stories and news seemed to get worse. Again, he felt very sad when he heard such news, and dreaded the thought of what might have happened to his parents. Nevertheless, he and his wife were determined to make a success of their circumstances. Although he could not put the war to one side— he was reminded of it every day at the clinic— being a dedicated doctor to all who required his services, he got on with his work and prayed that, in the end, things would get better. Time moved on and, every day, news came in about what was happening around the world, and very little of it was good news. Sometimes, his spirit was lifted when the 'Allies' had achieved some successful gains, but, on the whole, much of the news was not good.

* * *

Daniel, Druscilla and Arun had now been in the countryside for three months. While taking a ride in his neighbour's car every day, Daniel asked if he could try his hand at driving, so it was arranged that, while the children were in school, the neighbour's son, Joshua, would give him a lesson in his rest time, but only if the doctor could be spared the time. Daniel was now nearly thirty-two years old, and learnt very quickly how to drive. He had kept all this secret from his wife, and wanted to surprise her one day. Nearly two weeks later, he went with Joshua to a garage in the town, and they looked at a number of second-hand vehicles. A lot were in poor condition, but one or two looked better. The garage owner was an Arab. Joshua asked him what he wanted for the better looking car, and the Arab replied two hundred shekels. Joshua retorted that was a little too much and, after much talk between the two of them, they agreed on a price. Daniel has saved quite a sum of money, and had enough to cover the cost of the vehicle. He told the Arab he would pick the car up the next day, which was a Saturday. The next day, Joshua gave him a lift into town and took him to the garage. The car was standing there, and it looked a lot cleaner than it had the day before. Daniel greeted the Arab in Arabic and got into the car, watched by Joshua who, as Daniel started it up and jerkily drove away, had a big smile on his face. After a shaky start, Daniel was soon driving confidently, being a quick learner. Joshua got in his car and followed Daniel home. Arriving at his house, Daniel jumped out of the car and ran into the house, saying to his wife in an excited voice, "Come outside and see what I have for you and the family!"

Coming out of the doorway and seeing the car, she looked a little dumbfounded. She then asked how he came to have this car. He said he had kept it a secret from her, because he had wanted to surprise her and tell her that now he would be independent and they would all be able to travel as they wished. Life was now getting very settled, and Daniel was feeling more secure each day, having a very good job and the respect of the people he came into contact with. He enjoyed the friendship of his Jewish neighbours, and they often visited one another, especially on festival or religious occasions, although he had little contact with his religion in Russia, as there had been no synagogue where they lived and they had been the only Jewish family in the village.

* * *

One day, Daniel was at home when there was a knock on the door. He opened it and saw a Palestinian standing there. Daniel asked him if there was something he had come to see him about. The man started to speak in Arabic, but then stopped and started talking in English. Daniel had picked up English in the time he had been in Palestine, whilst working at the military hospital. The man

42

introduced himself as his Palestinian neighbour further down the hill, at the house where the big cedar tree stood with his land around with the olive trees and two hectares of land, on which he mostly grazed his few sheep and goats. He told Daniel that the previous owner of his house had let him graze his animals on his land for a small rent. He introduced himself to Daniel as Usef, and said he lived with his wife and elderly father. His mother had died three years ago. Apparently, she had become seriously ill, and the nearest doctor was in the town. Before they could get her there, she had died on the way. She was a Lebanese, from a Christian background, but his father was Palestinian. Usef asked why he had come to this house. The doctor replied that he liked the countryside and thought it would be a fine place to bring up his son, and his wife liked the countryside better than the town. Without giving an answer, Daniel said he would like to think about Usef's request and discuss it with his wife, and he would come to Usef's house in the morning and let him know if he would agree to his renting the land.

After talking with his wife about what the man had said, they both thought it would not be a bad idea to let him have the land. What could they do with four hectares? Plus, his work would not give him enough time to look after animals or even cultivate any of it.

In the morning, Daniel walked down the hill and took the boy with him. He entered into the courtyard of Usef's house and, as he did so, noticed how well kept it was, and the beautiful cedar tree made it appear more pleasant. Usef came out of the house with a broad smile on his face. The doctor had assumed, when he had first seen him, that his age was about twenty-five. It must have been due to Daniel's polite approach that Usef had a feeling the doctor was going to agree to his need. He was right, and he shook hands with Daniel and signed a rental agreement, at the same time saying he was not a rich man. He offered Daniel some tea and asked if he would come into the house and meet his family. Inside was very clean and orderly.

43

Sitting on a chair by a table was his father, an older man of about sixty, with a beard and quite a noble face. He was dressed in the usual Arabic clothes and headdress. By his side sat a pretty woman. Usef said, "This is my wife, Letitia."

She stood and gave a bow to Daniel, and then she approached the boy and said in Arabic what a fine looking boy he was. She looked quite young, and could not be more than twenty-two or so years old. Daniel said he had to go to work soon. As he was leaving, Usef told his wife that their neighbour was a doctor. Usef then brought the doctor's attention to his wife. With another smile, he indicated that his wife was expecting their first child in four to five months' time, and he hoped, like Daniel, he would have a fine-looking boy like his son. Usef walked with Daniel and Arun and, while doing so, said he had been born here and had met his wife, Letitia, while he had been visiting with his relatives in the Lebanon. His parents had lived outside Haifa on their farm all their lives, and had inherited it from their parents. His wife had been given a good education, and she was very bright academically, but, since his mother's death, they had had to come back home. Usef and Letitia looked after the house and farm with his father. He said, since they had been there, they had found their other neighbours in the Jewish houses quite friendly, but had very little contact with them, but they did have Palestinian friends living along the valley, who were mainly small farmers. Saying farewell to each other, Daniel set off back up the hill to his house, feeling quite happy. With all the tensions between Arabs, British and Jews, it was a relief to know that at least his Palestinian neighbours were friendly.

* * *

Although he and his wife were experiencing a fairly ordinary and even routine lifestyle, Daniel was very much aware of what was happening in the world around him. There had been a number of naval battles in the

44

Mediterranean. The Italians had been defeated in Africa, but the situation had since deteriorated. The Germans had a foothold in North Africa and were making a swift advance towards Egypt. His position in Palestine was not looking as secure as he had thought it was. The news seemed to get worse as the days went by. The British were suffering heavy losses at home, at sea and on the continent of Europe. Nevertheless, he had, as he reminded himself grimly on many occasions, left Russia to begin a new life and, like his father, he was dedicated to his work. He knew that nothing would be in his way to achieve his goal, and, as he had said before, he was a life saver, not a life taker, and believed that, whatever might happen around him, this would carry him through.

* * *

The days and months went past and the news never seemed to get any better, but life had to go on and, every day at the clinic, more and more casualties seemed to come in, not all of them caused by the war; quite a number were from terror attacks from both the Jewish and Palestinian groups who seemed to be opposed to each other over territory and ownership of the holy places, especially Jerusalem. Everyone, Catholics, Muslims, Jews, Coptics, and Anglicans all wanted a piece of it. It was hard to believe that each of them worshipped the same God, but could not agree with the principles of God.

After a hard day's work at the clinic, Daniel felt quite tired and upset a little by what he had to do there. He settled down, thankful to be home. He embraced the boy and put him on his knee, spoke to him and made him laugh. Their activities were abruptly halted when he heard a noise from outside. Daniel told his wife to hold the boy while he went outside to find out what and where the noise was. He opened the door and was confronted by Usef, his neighbour, in a distraught state, with his arms waving in all directions. He kept shouting at the doctor in Arabic, "Come

45

quickly; come quickly; the baby; the baby."

Daniel hurried inside, quickly picked up his medical bag, which he always kept by him, and said to his wife, "I have to go. Take care of the boy."

He followed Usef hurriedly down the hill. They got to the house and, with Usef leading, burst in, and, on a low bed, his wife looked in extreme pain. Daniel had experience with childbirth, but that was with his own wife, and villagers in Russia where he had lived and was trusted. Daniel was a little cautious. He had not attended to Arab women or other nationalities in this condition. He knew he had to do something quickly, and proceeded to give her an injection to ease her pain. Usef, meanwhile, was in a very nervous state. Uncertain how he would be accepted by Usef's wife, he told Usef to hurry back to his house and tell his wife to come down as fast as she could, and bring the boy with her. Usef was gone in a flash. A few minutes later, he appeared with Druscilla and the boy. Daniel told Usef and his father to leave the room and take the boy with them. Daniel said he knew what was wrong with Usef's wife. She was having great difficulty in giving birth, and would need a lot of help. As he was not familiar with Arab women, he told her that he would give his wife instructions to help her if she would approve. Being desperate and frightened, she nodded in agreement. Meanwhile, the doctor did what he could to help, getting water and comforting the woman.

Time was passing, and it seemed that nothing his wife did on his instructions had a result. In the other room, Usef, his father and the boy must have been wondering what was happening. Daniel called Usef to come and be with his wife. The doctor told Letitia that she would have to have another injection. He told Usef to hold and encourage her. Two and a half hours had gone past, and everyone was getting very worried, and the woman was crying out in pain. Daniel's wife kept encouraging her to try harder to release the baby. Suddenly, with a loud scream, the child appeared. Daniel's wife immediately helped to deliver it and, once the child was out, they washed and wrapped it. Usef's face was now lighted up. The baby was crying; his wife looked weak, but was smiling. Usef wanted to know whether the baby was a boy or a girl. Daniel's wife said it was a perfect little girl. It had taken nearly three hours for Usef's wife to give birth, and a feeling of relief had come over everyone. They told the doctor's wife, Druscilla, they would name the girl 'Ruth' in gratitude to them. Daniel and his wife said they would have to go take the boy to bed and rest themselves. Usef and his father were overcome with joy, and kept thanking the doctor and his wife for helping them. Without them, they might have lost the baby.

The next day, Daniel went, as usual, to work, but now he was driving himself and, although feeling exhausted after the previous night, he was in a very happy mood. As usual, he encountered the same depressing situations at the clinic. It seemed that, despite having to attend to war casualties, he was still appalled by the atrocities carried out by the clashes between the Palestinians on the Jews, and vice versa. The news, again, was quite depressing, and also worrying. It was now known that the Italian army had been defeated in Africa, but that the German army had made tremendous gains and had occupied France. This in itself was a disaster for his fellow Jews there. It was now that the Germans would take more revenge on the Jewish population who had not been able to get away. Also, the Germans had achieved a foothold in other parts, including the North African coast, and were building their forces there. He could only hope that something would happen to improve the situation, as the war did not seem to be going in favour of the Allies.

* * *

As the days went past, Daniel concentrated on his work and his family. His son, Arun, was nearly five years old, and would have to be educated. He made inquiries in the town, and found a Jewish school for Arun. Now, he

47

would be able to take the boy to school each day, but another problem had arisen. Although he had paid off his debt, the rabbi was more demanding that he attend the synagogue more often and help his son with his faith. This Daniel promised to do. The year was coming to an end, but not the violence at home and around the world. It was the end of November. Even the weather was depressing. It was cold and, at times, quite wet. December arrived and Christmas, which was widely celebrated by all the religions, especially in Jerusalem, the holiest of places to them all. Daniel, of course, had not travelled very far outside the area where he lived, and Jerusalem was some distance to the south, in the area where a lot of the trouble was being caused, but he did think that he would, one day, be able to go there, perhaps when the country and the world got back to normality. On December 7, 1941, bombs began to drop, literally, but not in Palestine. The news came through that the Japanese had attacked the American naval base at Pearl Harbour in the Pacific Islands. The Americans immediately declared war on Japan. Everybody was talking about it and believed that this could make a big difference in the Allies' favour, with the help that the Americans were in a position to give. A wave of optimism spread around, and everyone hoped the war would soon end. This optimism was short lived as the situation deteriorated in Europe, and it looked as though the German army was about to invade Russia.

*   *   *

When Daniel heard the news about the shock of the German invasion of the Soviet Union, it made him more depressed. What would happen to his parents, who were now in their sixties? Even if they had survived the Russian pogrom, they certainly would not survive the Nazis, with their cold hatred for the Jews and the Slavs. It was unbearable to him to think about it, and he blamed himself. Maybe, if the whole family had made the journey, it was

48

possible his parents may have survived. He felt very guilty about it, but his wife said that no matter how much he might have tried to convince his father, she knew he would not have left. He always said his patients were his priority, and that was what he was dedicated to. Now that the war had spread virtually around the world, what would be the result, and how long would it last? There were very few places in the world that were not being troubled by it. The Germans were now having setbacks with their campaigns. They had reached the outskirts of Egypt, but were being repulsed by the British and their allies. They were as near as Greece and Crete, within striking distance of Palestine. The naval forces in the Mediterranean had been able to repulse any advances. The German army had also suffered a great loss on the Russian front. The Americans were making progress against the Japanese. As the months went by, it seemed the news was beginning to get a little better. The year was now 1944, and the Allies were making good progress and winning back most of the territories that had been lost. The Russians were routing the Germans, and only those who had survived the fighting were being driven back to their homeland. The war seemed to be coming to an end. The situation was deteriorating in other aspects. In Palestine, there seemed to be more anger against British rule and certain groups, like the Zionists, were creating disorder in many parts of the country. There were calls now for a 'State of Israel'. This was causing more tension with the Palestinians, who believed Palestine belonged to them. Daniel now questioned, in his mind, where he belonged. He had come to Palestine for a new life, but that was not happening. He got on well with all he met and was, as a doctor, quite respected by all who knew him. After all, his wife was not fully Jewish; she was of a mixture from her parents. Her mother was Jewish, but her father was a Polish Catholic and, as a result, Daniel was in a position of not knowing whose side he was really on. As the year progressed, Daniel carried on with his life with his family as well as was possible. In spite of all the troubles and depressing news that had dogged him in the last years, he still had enough optimism left in him to think that life would get better.

* * *

It was now well into the year 1944, and the wearying conflict was at last going rather better for the Allies, who were now forcing the enemy back throughout Europe, Africa and the Mediterranean. The Russians were retaking their land, and the Germans appeared to be on the verge of defeat. Italy had ceased to fight on the Axis side in September 1943, but had been occupied by German forces. Allied armies had landed on the Italian mainland, but were still finding stiff opposition from the Germans, who had taken over Rome. Their resistance was proving a very tough and costly operation. It was not until the next year, in May 1945, that the Germans finally surrendered. Also, in the Low Countries, Allied successes seemed to trigger other Axis combatants to declare ceasefires. At last, there seemed to be a glimmer of hope that the world would return to a normal existence. There was still a war going on in the Pacific, but, like many people in Europe and the Levant, this was not foremost on Daniel's mind. Japan was a long way from Palestine. Now was the time to consolidate his life and settle into a more peaceful existence with his wife and son, Arun. He saw his neighbour, Usef, quite often, as he tended his goats and sheep on the land that Daniel had rented to him. They discussed the news, and he always told the doctor how his daughter, Ruth, was doing. Although he would really have liked a boy, he was happy that the doctor had helped to give them a beautiful little girl, also saying that his wife, Letitia, was very well.

The war was still going on in the Far East, but was abruptly terminated by the Americans dropping atomic bombs on Hiroshima and Nagasaki on August 6 and 9, 1945. The results were catastrophic and horrific. Never had any country been so devastated. As pictures were released, Daniel was shocked, and could not believe that human beings could do this to their fellow man, but others had a different view, saying the Japanese had not been humane in dealing with their enemies.

*   *   *

Another year was coming to a close, but it had not been as peaceful as had been hoped. Nations everywhere were making demands and changes. The United Nations had been set up, and the League of Nations had been wound up. Now that another New Year was in prospect, at Christmas, it was quite calm, and it had given people time to reflect now the war was over. Nations had to re-establish themselves, but there was a lot of tension amongst some of the smaller ones. There were a lot of diplomatic talks and dialogue going on. Daniel wondered what the future was going to be. He was still doing his work at the clinic, but, fortunately, the casualties were getting fewer. He now had to deal a lot more with the flood of immigrants that were arriving daily, some in a terrible state. They had arrived by all manner of means. The British Royal Navy was intercepting many of the larger boats. Some had so many on board as to make them so low in the water that they could sink, drowning the hundreds that were on board, many of them women and children. The numbers were increasing daily and, despite all the effort to stop them, many thousands made it to Palestine. This flood of humanity was now creating a greater potential for disaster. Palestinians became more alarmed at the new wave of Jewish refugees. They began to take their revenge, not only on the refugees and other Jewish communities, but also on the British. Over the next four months, more and more Jewish refugees arrived in the land. Some were from countries that had not been troubled by the war. These people were not poor, and a lot had ambitions to settle there and prosper. The more refugees that arrived, the more the

Palestinians resented them. On July 22, 1946, the British HQ in Jerusalem was blown up. The Palestinians were seeing the situation as a numbers solution. The more Jewish refugees who settled, the less chance there was of the Palestinians having a Palestine nation. Meanwhile, all over Europe and the Western world, governments and leaders were changing. Although Daniel was aware of what was happening elsewhere, the situation here was precarious. Jewish and Arab parties were causing a great amount of terrorism. As the year went on, political parties began to emerge, and these even caused more trouble because of alliances with other countries. 1946 had been another year of uncertainty.

A Palestine Committee had been formed and, on August 29, 1947, they agreed that the British Mandate should end. A majority report recommended Partition. When he heard about this, Daniel thought it might be the best solution— little did he know how this was going to affect him and his family in the future. Daniel was even more optimistic when it was announced from the UN Assembly that the Palestine Committee voted in favour of the Partition of Palestine into separate Jewish and Arab states. At last, it seemed that the solution had been found to settle the land of Palestine. This could have been the start of a new beginning for all the people, refugees and Arabs alike, but, unfortunately, this would not happen. In the Jewish community, some of their leaders were against the settlement, as were some hard-line Palestinians, who were being supported by outside influences. This led to more violence and bloodshed. Numbers of Jews started encroaching on what was Palestinian land, and depriving the occupants of their legitimate territory, many of whom had titles to their land, but this was ignored. The worst was to happen on May 14, 1948. The British Mandate in Palestine ended at midnight and, at the same time, the Jewish leaders and community declared a new 'State of Israel'. There were quite a number of ministers in the new state who raised their objections to a 'fait accompli' solution and thought that the agreements previously passed were the best for the Arabs and the Jews, but rightwing hard-liners in the Likud Party did not want to listen. Daniel and his wife and son, Arun, knew that they could not help, and could do nothing more than carry on as normal a life as possible.

*   *   *

Usef, the Palestinian neighbour, seemed not to involve himself in the politics and fighting, and was always polite and friendly to the doctor and his family. He had let Arun, who was now ten years old, join him to herd his sheep and goats, which Arun loved doing, and he would sometimes sit with Usef, his wife and the girl, Ruth, who was now five years old. When his father had brought him back from school, he would hurriedly go down the road to Usef's house to help with milking the goats, and Letitia would give him and the girl a drink of the milk. Everything seemed to be in a state of change around the world and, even though the war was over, some countries were suffering more hardships than before. There were shortages of goods and food. It was not easy to transport much by cargo boats. The Suez Canal had been blocked by sunken ships during the war, and would take a long time to re-open again. Meanwhile, in the New State of Israel, there was much controversy about what was going on, and, in places further away like Jerusalem, it was causing great problems for all the religious who, for centuries, had worshipped there. Violence was flaring up most days with Arabs attacking Jews and vice versa. It was a little fortunate that, in the area where Daniel lived, it was much more sporadic. Most of the refugees that had landed in Israel had dissipated into the community, and numbers of them had formed co-operatives or kibbutz where they lived together and helped to grow food and look after each other.

*   *   *

53

As time passed, more and more land was being illegally taken by the Jews from the Palestinian occupants. This was being condoned by the government, who turned a blind eye to it, and now Israel had formed a strong army and police force, who were, at times, instrumental in helping to expel the Palestinians who, by and large, were just poor peasant farmers eking out a living. Daniel knew that, by displacing these people, it was going to cause much more trouble and would not endear the Arabs to the Jews. Refugee camps were springing up all over Palestine near some of the main cities and towns. The people there suffered terribly. They had virtually no amenities or sanitation, and no medical help. Some of the displaced Palestinians had fled to the Lebanon or Jordan, where more refugee camps were being set up. Daniel and his family had managed to avoid any aggression, as now he was recognised for what he was— a doctor— and was treated with respect. He was very open-minded and, in spite of what was going on around him, stuck to his principles and treated everyone the same. Although he had been born a Jew, he was not as dogmatic and unbending as some of his contemporaries. Like his parents, he had a great respect for his fellow men, irrespective of their nationality. So far, this had made his life more normal, and he was not living in fear, especially seeing what was happening in other parts of Israel.

For a while, it seemed that what was happening in Israel had more or less been forgotten by the rest of the world. Except for one or two terrorist attacks on important places or people, Palestine was not making the news. It was now 1956 and, suddenly, the world was alerted to an attack by the Israelis on Egypt. They overwhelmed the Egyptians with their superior armaments in a war lasting five days, taking Sinai and a considerable amount of territory. In the intervening years, the Israelis had built up a large army, largely through conscription. They had been heavily supported by the American and European arms dealers, who supplied most of their weapons. They were now seeking expansion, to the wrath of the Arabs. Israel had started to become more prosperous and was being helped, not only by the Americans, but also prosperous expatriates, and a lot of Jewish refugees had become rich since the Second World War. This was a great disadvantage to the Palestinian Arabs who, generally, were a poor nation.

Daniel's son, Arun, was now eighteen years old, and had been through the rituals required of a Jewish boy and, still with his family, he was friendly with his Palestinian neighbour, Usef, and spent his leisure time now and again visiting them and sitting under the big cedar tree, talking. Arun had become quite fluent in Arabic from his education. He also spoke Russian and Hebrew. Usef's little girl, Ruth, was growing, too, and was now twelve years old, and it was obvious that she would be a beautiful woman. She had the good looks of her Lebanese mother. They all appeared to be happy and getting on with life, but were still aware of what was happening in the country. Having more or less finished his education, Arun was considered by his teachers to be a bright and intelligent person. His father and mother were very pleased with their son, and had hoped he would study to be a doctor like his father but, for the moment, that was out of the question. Arun, at eighteen years old, had to do his conscription in the Israeli army, and would soon be leaving home to be sent up country to a training base just outside the Lebanese border with Israel. His father and mother were not too happy when hearing this. Reports coming from there were not good. There were many Palestinian refugees in camps in the south of the country, and it was considered a volatile area. The day came when Arun said goodbye to his mother and father. It was very painful for his parents, his father especially, as he had left his parents in Russia, and to add to his worries, he had no idea what had happened to them. Daniel said he would take Arun to the conscription centre, but Arun said an army vehicle would soon be there to take him. Very soon, it appeared. Inside were several other conscripts. Arun gripped his father's hand and hugged him, and then put his arms around his mother and kissed her. He loved her very much. She had always made certain everything was done for him. She had never complained when things went wrong, kept the house in order, and had always been happy with his father. They were both devoted to each other. Arun finally left, waving farewell to his parents. On the way down the hill, he asked the driver to stop at Usef's farm. He got out and Usef came to greet him with Letitia and Ruth. They said a few words, and Arun looked a little longer at Ruth, who smiled and held out her hand to him. He gently shook it, and it was obvious their parting had an emotional effect on him. He knew he had a liking for her. Arun returned to the vehicle and, as it started off, he looked back; he could see his parents standing outside the house. Usef and his wife were also waving him away until he was out of sight.

*   *   *

The Aserovs were now without their son, and it would feel quite empty without him. Also, the Usef family would miss Arun. He had spent a lot of time with them. Ruth was now at school in the town. She travelled on the bus that still came through every day. Apart from what was going on in the outside world, the Aserovs and Usef's family carried on with their daily work, Usef with his farm, and the doctor at the clinic. With Arun now in the army, Daniel and Druscilla had a lot more time to think of things and wondered, at times, what their future held. Daniel was now forty-six years old, and hoped he would still be able to carry on with his work at the clinic, which had been a godsend to him, as now he was better off and could have a few more little luxuries. Having the car, he often went to the synagogue. Although he was quite a liberal Jew, he had a great respect for his religion. He was welcomed by the rabbi when he went to worship. This, of course, pleased the rabbi, as Daniel had, in the past, said he would make an effort to attend.

The years were passing quite quickly, and everywhere in the world change was taking place. Some nations were allying with others. Treaties were being signed by groups of people and countries that had something in common with each other. Some countries wanted independence and, although Israel was, or seemed to be, more stable with its government, it was still experiencing some runaway acts of terrorism. This was mainly fuelled by the Jewish population taking over Palestinian land and ejecting the residents. There had been cases of Palestinian snipers firing into Jewish houses and killing some of the occupants. This made matters worse, and retaliation followed by the army, with their vehicles, firepower and tear gas. The shooting came mostly from small Palestinian villages in the valleys, and was aimed at the new Jewish settlements that had been built on Palestinian land above them. It seemed the pattern in which these settlements were built was to dominate, in lots of cases overlooking the small villages. Of course, the Palestinians deeply resented losing their homes, gardens and grazing land for their animals, especially the families that had been forceably ejected from them. The land had been in their families for many generations. Before the Second World War, when the British had a mandate, they had no problems, except that they did not like the British, or any other nation, for that matter, telling them what to do and were going to resist the Jews taking over their homes. They, like most reasonable and peaceful people, only wanted their gardens and their life back. As time went on— it was now 1962— it did not get any better; The Israeli government was being heavily supported with arms and finance by the Americans and wealthy Jewish businessmen who were financing many projects, who were mostly, again, coming from other countries.

Usef, too, was worried by what was happening. Fortunately, his daughter, Ruth, had finished her primary education. She was now eighteen years old and had adopted a Western lifestyle in clothes that showed her off to be a beautiful and intelligent woman, with dark brown hair and an elegant figure. She had acquired a place at a Jewish college in Haifa, and was studying to be a teacher.

Five years had passed, and Arun, much to his father's dismay, after serving his time as a conscript, had made a decision to stay in the army. He had proved to his superiors that he was a capable soldier, and was a very good organiser. He was now stationed in an area around Jerusalem. Although he had made many visits to his parents' home, he had not seen Usef's daughter, Ruth, for a long time, but, by accounts from his parents, she had become a beautiful and attractive woman.

Daniel was still very friendly with his Arab neighbours, but this was to change one day. A sniper had fired into his Jewish neighbours' houses, and had wounded one of the occupants. This had caused outrage and, believing the firing had come from the Arab village in the valley, it was not long before a unit of the Israeli army arrived in the village and started to interrogate the occupants. None of the villagers would say or tell where or who had fired at the houses. A group of Palestinians consisting of men and boys then started throwing stones and objects at the army patrol. It was then the vehicles turned and left, at the same time firing shots and tear gas. Daniel and his wife found this episode disturbing, and hoped it would not occur again. He discussed the incident with his fellow doctors at the clinic, and was told that the local Arabs were being encouraged to put up more resistance to the Israelis by outside rebel groups, who were encouraging disillusioned Palestinians, determined to repossess their land and gardens. It was in their blood to regain their territories. After all, like their ancestors, they were agriculturalists and horticulturists. They had survived for centuries like this, and had a peaceful existence, even with the Jewish population already living there, whose people were probably the descendants of the Israelites who had invaded Palestine in around 1250 BC and determined

Jerusalem to be their sanctuary, a Holy Place and a capital, before the birth of Christ. Jerusalem has been fought for and has continued to be a bone of contention to this day. Who had the right to it— the Jews or Arabs? The Balfour Declaration in 1917 recognised a home for the Jews. The British had occupied Palestine, and Jerusalem had been taken. After the Second World War had ceased, Palestine was to be cursed with unrest, and was becoming more so from year to year. It often went through Daniel's mind— had he become trapped in a never-ending cycle of hate and violence, not only from Palestinians, but from his own kind, and he worried more and more about his son, Arun, who was now permanently part of it. There was nothing he could do about it, but take things as they came from day to day. At times, when he was at home with his wife, he would sit and wonder if things might have been different had he not left Russia, but, on reflection, he could not have done anything differently. Not knowing what had happened to his parents still ran through his mind. They would be quite old. Perhaps they could have died or may have suffered the fate of millions of Jews sent to gulags or to death camps in Europe. The thought was unbearable to him. As the days went past, he would receive a letter from Arun, which lifted his spirit, and his son would visit at times. This made him happy. He had a feeling of pride for Arun, seeing him in his uniform, no longer an ordinary soldier, but an officer. Arun would always ask if they had seen Ruth, and was very interested in how she was. Unconsciously, he had formed a bond with her from his young days. Leaving his parents was always a painful process, especially as the violence was increasing from the north to the south of the country.

CHAPTER III
Birth, Death & Marriage

One bright spring day, Daniel had been to the synagogue, which gave him a sense of hope and a much better feeling. However, his mood changed abruptly on arriving back home, where he found Usef looking very distressed, talking to Druscilla. When Usef saw Daniel, he ran towards him and, talking rapidly in Arabic, asked the doctor if he would come quickly to his house. He said his father was very ill. With that, the doctor got his bag and hurried down the hill with Usef. The old man was lying on a bed in a small room, looking very pale and weak. The doctor took the old man's hand, felt his pulse, and looked at his eyes. He turned to Usef and Letitia and, with his head a little low, shook it and gave the old man a small injection of pain killer. He then moved away from the bed and told Usef that his father was dying, and there was nothing he could do, but he would not be suffering, as, with the small dose of pain killer, he would feel no pain. Daniel left them after expressing his sympathy, took his leave and went back home. By the look on his face, his wife knew it was not good news.

The next morning, Usef visited the doctor's house and gave him the news that the old man had died about an hour or so after he had left, and he told Daniel that now he would go make arrangements for the funeral. He would be buried along with the other members of his family at the graveyard in the village, down below in the valley. Everything was not going emotionally well for Daniel and, to make matters worse, his Jewish neighbours were not pleased with him attending to Palestinians, although he did this almost every day at the clinic. His neighbours thought it wrong, as they, the Arabs, had attacked them with sniper fire and wounded some of them. Daniel said that Usef had not harmed them. Now was the time for thinking what he should do. It seemed that all his intentions at helping his fellow men appeared so counter productive in that every day at the clinic, while he was helping patients to get better and saving lives each day, there was more killing going on from both sides. There had been more sniper fire into the little Jewish settlement near Daniel's house. It was very worrying to him and, although it seemed that he was never a target, he put it down to the fact that Usef probably had some influence over this.

*   *   *

Nevertheless, Daniel decided to have a discussion with his wife about the situation. They sat one evening and talked it over. After a short discussion, they agreed that perhaps they would be safer in the town, in the mainly Jewish quarter, which was now quite large and becoming quite prosperous. They decided that now was the time to move, before it got much worse. The next day, Daniel went to see an agent and told him he was looking for a house in the town. With the influx of refugees that had arrived in the past, there were many new houses that had been built, even some on land once owned by Palestinians that had been purchased legally from them. The agent told Daniel he would find him a house as soon as he could. Daniel was now desperate to move. He could not believe how distressing it was to be in a country that was called the 'Promised Land', but which offered so little promise to him. This was not what he had expected when he first arrived, also finding that the problems were self-made by the Palestinians and his own people. Even in the government, there were arguments about how the situation should be solved. Some members of the parliament came up in favour of the Partition of the country, and others were very much against it. He had been very relieved when the Palestinian idea of partition was put forward, and had looked forward to having a settled life for his wife and family. It turned out that the situation was not getting any better, and things were about to get worse, much worse.

*　*　*

The year was now 1967 and, on June 5, the world woke up to hear that the Israeli army had invaded Sinai, the West Bank of Palestine, the Gaza Strip, together with the Golan Heights in Syria, and had appropriated land that was occupied by Palestinians. This caused an outrage, especially as a peace treaty had been in force. Friends of Israel were dismayed by the action of the Israelis. This incursion had outraged the Palestinians, who now had no alternative but to declare a Holy War or Jihad on their enemy. The Palestinians had really no option on how to get their land back but by armed struggle. They were at a disadvantage with this, as the Israeli army was heavily superior and was being armed and supported again by the Americans, who had flooded weapons on them, whereas the Palestinians had little or no support from the wealthy Arab, Islamic countries. The action taken by the army gave Daniel more to worry about. No doubt his son was involved in it, too. With all the protests and opinions of nations, the Israelis were not going to yield or retreat from their goal; to rid Palestine of its Arab inhabitants. Daniel felt he was not in any position for solving these problems, so had to concentrate on his life as best he could. The agent whom he had asked to find a house in the town gave him the news that he had found a house for him. If he liked it, he could purchase it. The next day, he left the clinic where he was still working and, with the agent, went to look at the house. It was typical of the new houses that had been built. After having a look around, Daniel thought it would suit them, at least for the time being, and hoped his wife would like it. The day came when he was moving and, in the meantime, he had collected his possessions together. Usef, his neighbour, was quite upset that he was leaving. Although Daniel had told him that the reason for their leaving was to be close to his work at the clinic, Daniel, of course, knew this was not really the reason. Usef said he would help them move, which Daniel thanked him for. Usef said he could find transport from the village to take anything that he could not take in his car. Having arrived at the new house, Usef helped to unload and carry the furniture and other items into the house. Before getting into the truck, he put his arms around Daniel, hugged him, then bowed to Druscilla and left, saying that he hoped he would see him again, and would always be grateful to him for helping with the birth of his lovely daughter, Ruth, who had grown up to be an intelligent and beautiful woman.

*   *   *

Ruth had been away in Jerusalem now for three years, and had finished her course. She was now in the position to get a job at a school. She went home to see her parents, and was surprised to find that her neighbour, Daniel, had moved to the town. Daniel's house was occupied by another Jewish family. Her father, Usef, told her why the doctor had moved. She asked what had happened to Arun— where was he now, and what was he doing? Ruth knew he had been conscripted, but nothing more. She seemed to show a kind of sadness in her face, then she smiled and started telling her parents how she had got on in Jerusalem, which she said was a very divided city, but she had found it quite interesting. It seemed that there was a lot of dissention amongst the inhabitants. Nevertheless, there were some very good schools there, and she hoped she would be able to teach in one.

Having been home for a few days, Ruth had a feeling of loneliness. She was thinking of the times she and

Arun used to play and look after the animals. She had to know what had happened to him, and the only way was to ask his father. She asked her father where the doctor lived, and he told her. She decided she would go that day, as she would have to go back to Jerusalem for interviews at some of the schools she had seen. She went to the town, to the doctor's house, and knocked on the door, whereupon Daniel's wife, Druscilla, opened the door, and was a little taken aback seeing this beautiful woman standing there. Druscilla had not seen a great deal of Ruth since she left for college. Ruth introduced herself, at which point the doctor's wife remembered her, remarked how she looked and asked her politely how old she was now, as it seemed such a long time that she had seen her. Ruth said she was now twenty-three years old. She asked Druscilla what Arun was doing now, and Druscilla replied that he was in the Israeli army and had officer rank, adding, "We don't see him very often, as he is always moving about in different areas, as the troubles continue."

Ruth thanked her and asked her to remember her to the doctor, said goodbye, and left.

The next day, Ruth left home to catch a bus back to Jerusalem. There had been quite a lot of trouble in and around the city, with terrorist attacks by various groups from different parties, some calling themselves by different names. It was about a hundred and fifty kilometres south of Haifa, and some of the trouble places and refugee camps were in that area. Ruth had experienced no problem going up to see her parents, so was not unduly worried. People lived every day in fear, and it just seemed to be a way of life with both Jews and Palestinians. Ruth was aware that, after the recent war and takeover of Palestinian land, it would cause more resentment towards the Jews. Ruth, like her father, Usef, was a moderate person, and had to be in a non-collaborative position if she wanted to achieve her ambitions to teach. She did have some advantage through her parents, who had a mixed background of Arab and Christian.

On her way to Jerusalem, the bus was stopped by an army patrol of tanks and vehicles; they were approaching a refugee camp that had been quiet for some time, but, apparently, fighting had now broken out. Some Israeli soldiers had been wounded, and a Palestinian had been fatally shot. There were crowds of people around, some of them young, throwing missiles at the soldiers. Ruth had experienced scenes of violence in Jerusalem on a number of occasions, but had not been embroiled in it. Soldiers told everyone to get off the bus and produce their passes. One or two officers were checking them. One of the officers asked Ruth for her pass. On seeing it, he suddenly looked at her face, then appeared to be a little surprised. He asked, "Are you Usef's daughter?"

She looked at him, equally surprised, and said, "Yes, that's right."

"What are you doing on the bus?" the officer asked.

Ruth replied, "I'm going back to Jerusalem, where I have a little apartment. I have just finished my studies to be a teacher, and hope to get a job at one of the schools there."

The officer said, "Perhaps you do not recognise me."

Ruth replied, "You are Arun, Doctor Aserov's son."

He nodded, took a pad from his pocket, and wrote something in it. He gave the note to Ruth with her pass, then announced in a loud voice, "Right, everyone can get back on the bus."

The bus, in the meantime, had been searched. Ruth gave a little smile, but Arun just kept a straight face and showed no sign of emotion. In the bus, Ruth wanted to look at the note Arun had written, but thought it better to wait until the privacy of her flat.

When she arrived, she hurriedly opened the note that Arun had given her, and in it was an address in Jerusalem. Ruth's heart began to pound. What did she have to do? Did he mean that he would like her to visit him? Ruth had known in her heart she had a great liking for Arun when she was younger. Now he must be at least twenty-nine years old, and handsome, to boot. No time had been given on the note Arun had handed to Ruth. The house address he had hurriedly scribbled on the paper was not in the City of Jerusalem, but some miles outside, in an area occupied mostly by Arabs. Ruth was uncertain what to do, but was so eager to see Arun again that she had to go. She could not take a taxi or have anyone to drive her to the address, as she knew by the furtive manner in which Arun had compiled the note, it was obvious he did not want anyone to see him with whom people might assume was a Palestinian woman, although Ruth always wore Western styled clothes.

There was a bus that would take her into the area. She took it to the place mentioned, so that she could then find the location discreetly. Approaching the address, she immediately realised that it was a military position, as there were soldiers around with their vehicles. She went towards the building, which looked very much like a normal house. At the door stood a soldier, who appeared to be on guard. He asked her in English if she wanted to see someone. She replied in English— her teaching studies had included English— and said she had come to see the officer in charge, and had an appointment with him. At that, the soldier opened the door.

Ruth entered the building and walked up a small flight of steps to a room. She knocked gently on the door, and a voice said, "Come in."

She opened the door and there, sitting at a desk, was Arun in his uniform. They looked at each other. Arun then got up, reached for a chair, and asked her to sit. For a while, they were both silent, then Arun asked Ruth where she lived and how her parents were. She replied that they were well, but that she did not see them as much as she would like, being in Jerusalem. She asked him how he had been and if he liked being in the army.

"Yes," he said, but added that he did not like the violence that was going on.

In the army, it was his job to try to keep the peace,

but this was not easy, and he sometimes felt that some of the tasks he was ordered to do did upset him. He then changed the subject and started to talk about the times when they were younger, and how he used to love tending the goats and sheep on her parents' land. Ruth smiled and said she, too, remembered those times. She then said that the area where her father lived had been having some trouble from the village below, but nothing had happened to them. She also said that her grandfather had died. He said he had heard that from his father. Ruth looked down, and said, "I should be going. Tomorrow, I have an interview for a place at a school."

Arun got up from his chair, went over to Ruth, put his hand out to her, and helped her out of her seat. As they stood together, he rang a bell to summon the guard outside, who quickly came in. He told him to go tell one of the soldiers with a vehicle to bring it to the outside of the building. The soldier left, and it seemed that Arun was not going to release his hand from hers. A feeling was coming over her, and she knew that not only had she had a great liking for Arun when she was younger, but now she was sure she was close to falling in love with him. Just then, the soldier appeared. Arun said, "The vehicle will take you back to town, but get off before you get to your flat. For the time being, this will be the best course."

He watched Ruth get into the vehicle, and gazed as it disappeared out of sight.

* * *

Ruth kept her appointment the next day. She tried to take her mind off the day before. It was important that she secured the post at the school. It was in her favour that she was multi-lingual, as the school was situated in the centre part of Jerusalem, between the Arab eastern section and the Jewish quarter. She hoped that she would secure a teaching post. This was a private school and taught language and academics to different nationalities, mostly sons and daughters of wealthy business and trades people. Ruth attended her interview at the time mentioned. She was interviewed by a man who asked her what her nationality was and why she wanted to work at the school. She said she was from a family where her father was Palestinian and her mother was from a Christian Lebanese family. They had sacrificed a great deal to give her a good education, for which she was most grateful, and wished to use it to help others. The man asked her if her family had ever experienced any problems with the people with whom she had associated. She replied that the college principal in the city where she had completed her studies said she had mixed with different nationalities and had always been accepted as an equal. Ruth was told to leave the room and to wait outside. After some time, which, to her, seemed an eternity, the man appeared and said that he would let her know the result of her interview by letter. Ruth thanked the man and left. She was now beginning to get worried about the outcome. Perhaps, because she was part Palestinian, this may go against her. Also, Arun was constantly on her mind. She could not forget him, and wondered if she would ever see him again.

Ruth went home to her small apartment, sat down and felt very depressed. At her age, it was vital she had work. Usef, her father, had helped her when she was being educated, and she knew her parents were not rich, or even well off. They had sacrificed a lot to support her. She felt she should now be able to help them and pay back something to them. While studying, in her spare time, Ruth had taken a job serving in a small restaurant, which was owned by a Greek. The money she had earned there was only enough to support her, so she knew she must have other work. Quite a number of days went past, and she had heard nothing.

It had been some time since she had been home to Haifa, and she was wondering how her parents were getting on. The doctor was no longer there, and she wondered if their new neighbours were friendly. Ruth woke up early the

68

next morning, feeling very low and anticipating the arrival of the post, and wondering if there was going to be a letter. She didn't have to wait long before a knock came at the door. She opened the door and was handed a letter. She was quite excited; this must be the response to her interview, she thought. On opening the letter, she was initially crestfallen, as it was not from the school, but from Arun. Her heart missed a beat or two, then she began to read it. It just asked if she would meet him at a certain time at a café in the Jewish quarter, and was signed 'Arun Aserov'. Ruth was a little taken aback at such a short note. It seemed more like an order than a romantic letter. Nevertheless, she still had an air of expectancy and excitement. Arun knew that Ruth would look right for him as, since she had left home to study, she had never worn Arab dress, only Western clothes. These made her acceptable to all the people she had encountered.

*　*　*

The day came when Ruth prepared herself to meet Arun, and she felt a little nervous about what would happen. She walked up to the café and saw Arun sitting there in his uniform, looking very smart. He got up and welcomed her with a gentle handshake, then took a chair and motioned her to sit. Arun asked her if she would like a cup of coffee, and she said she would. Then he summoned a waiter and asked him to bring the coffee and a drink of juice for himself. Arun began by asking her how her family was keeping. She said they were well. She, in turn, enquired of his father and mother. He said he had not seen them for some time, as his orders had kept him moving around various trouble spots, but he had received letters from them, and they were quite well, but his father was not happy with the situation in the country.

Arun and Ruth talked for a while, with small talk about the weather and music and how they hoped the troubles would go away and everyone could get on with their lives. Arun said he must say goodbye to her as he had to return to his military post, saying that he may be away for a few days, depending on the problems he had to try to solve. He said he would let Ruth know when he could see her again, if she was agreeable, to which she smiled and nodded. They both then took leave of each other, Arun not showing any emotion, but Ruth was shaking a little. Although she was now feeling elated at meeting Arun, the issue of the teaching post was still on her mind.

A few days later, a letter arrived for her. Thinking it would be from Arun, she suddenly remembered the job interview, and realised it was from the school. She tore the envelope open as quickly as she could and read the contents. Yes! She had got the post, and had instructions to start at the beginning of the next term, in two weeks' time. Life was beginning to look better, and she had a feeling of calm and happiness, but still could not get Arun off her mind, and what his intentions were. She would now tell her parents the good news, which would please them very much. The next time she saw Arun, she would let him know, too.

*   *   *

Daniel and Druscilla had settled into their new house, and he carried on every day with his work at the clinic. The casualties were not coming to the extent that they had in the recent Six-Day War, but there were incidents between hard-line Jews and Arabs, some of whom were not from Palestine, but were infiltrators from other Islamic countries. Most of the fighting was in areas to the south of the country, mainly in the occupied zones, which seemed to have been turned into a 'running sore' of hatred and mistrust. Daniel was a man of compassion and a liberal thinker; otherwise, he could never have been a doctor. The situation continually worried him, and Druscilla kept telling him they could do nothing about it. The people in power were the only ones, but they were too introverted and unyielding for compromise, so the situation would continue on both sides. Daniel remarked that they had been fortunate; at least they were alive and were a family, which was not the case with a lot of people in the country, especially the Palestinians. Although he loved his son, Arun, he had a feeling of disquietude with how the military reacted. Daniel and his wife often discussed happenings taking place around the world, and thought with dread what might have happened to them if they had not left Russia. With the news that daily came out from Europe, they would have either been killed or sent to slave camps in Siberia. He and Druscilla had given up thinking what might have been their fate. As both their parents in Poland and Russia had been in their fifties when they had left at the end of 1937, it was right to think they would have died or have suffered a worse fate, and would not have survived. Daniel's dream of a new life with his family was turning out to be a nightmare. Unlike Daniel in the Bible, he could not interpret dreams; otherwise, he would be in a different place and situation and, perhaps, could have foreseen what the future would be. Like every Jewish person of faith, he believed in the Promised Land, but, as the violence continued unabated, Israel, the 'Land of Milk and Honey' was quickly transforming into a land of 'Blood and Tears'.

* * *

Ruth, who was now teaching at the school, was getting on well. She was highly intelligent, and her pupils had a great respect for her. Besides, she was very good looking, and that was another of her assets. Her mind was always focussed on Arun; she had not heard from him for nearly a month, and was worried. By the nature of his position, he may have come to some harm. She was delighted, a few days later, to hear from him, asking if he could come to see her in her apartment on a certain day. Ruth was overcome with joy and relief. She was eager to

71

see him again, and could not wait to tell him about the teaching post at the school. She took it for granted that Arun did not need a reply and, in any case, she did not know the addresses for any military posts.

The day arrived when Arun was due. Ruth waited with excitement for a knock on the door. Exactly at the appointed time he had put in his letter, a rap on the door announced his arrival. On hearing Ruth's voice calling, Arun entered the room. For a moment, Ruth gave a little gasp. Arun was not in his uniform, but in civilian clothes. He went up to Ruth and gave her a kiss on the side of each cheek. The blood rushed through her veins and, feeling a little shocked, she composed herself and asked Arun to take a seat. Then she asked him if he would like a drink, saying she had tea, coffee, and orange juice. She said she did not keep alcohol in the house. Arun said he would have coffee, as he did not touch alcohol, because he had to have a clear head to administer or take charge of situations, and alcohol dulls your thinking. They both sat and talked whilst taking their drinks. Ruth asked him if he had experienced any problems while he had been away, but Arun did not seem to be listening. She could see that his eyes never seemed to leave her. She tried again to start a conversation by telling him that she had been given the teaching post at the school. He seemed to take notice of this, congratulated her, and said how lucky they were to have such a beautiful teacher. They talked about a few mundane things, then Arun looked at his watch and said he had to have an early night, as, first thing in the morning, he had to move down country to a place where things were bad. He would keep in touch with her as often as he could, and let her know when he would be able to see her again. Ruth thanked him for coming, and enquired why he was not in uniform. He replied that he could be a target for a disgruntled citizen, being alone in uniform. He would be vulnerable. He then took Ruth by the hand, gently pulled her closer, and kissed her on the lips for a brief moment. He apologised nervously, saying goodbye at the same time. Ruth said he had no need to apologise.

She was not embarrassed. He then went out of the door, looking back at Ruth and, as he left, he looked very happy and, for the first time, appeared to show some emotion. Ruth was in a daze. It seemed so sudden, but she had always known that one day she would see him again. It had to be fate that had made it happen. She was very excited by her experience. She felt quite elated, and pursued her teaching with renewed vigour with the thought that she was to see Arun again.

* * *

On one of her days off from teaching, Ruth decided to go visit her parents, Usef and Letitia. It had been some time since she had seen them; besides, she was eager to tell them about her new work, and also her meeting with Arun. As she did before, she took a bus, and, although buses had been attached by terror groups and the new phenomenon, the suicide bomber, she felt it would not happen on the bus she took. The passengers were mainly women and children who had been visiting or shopping. It stopped at some of the refugee camps, and this made her feel sad, as these people had been displaced, or even ejected, from their land and homes, and now were intent on taking revenge, which was aimed at the Jewish community. Recently, buses carrying Jewish workers and women had been blown up with horrific consequences. Daniel had not encountered such carnage. Fortunately, the area around Haifa was not targeted as other places like Hebron, Gaza and the Lebanese border.

Arriving at her father's house, Ruth was welcomed with open arms as if she had been lost. They were pleased to see her and to know that she was well. Usef and Letitia were delighted to hear of her success in getting the teaching post at the school, and she told them what her teaching duties were. Then, a little nervously, she told them about Arun and what he was doing, and intimated to them that she was in love with him, and she thought, by his manner,

73

that he felt the same, but she was not absolutely sure. She said they were to meet again when he returned from one of his patrols. Usef was a little surprised. All along, he had known Ruth and Arun had a liking for each other when they were younger. When Arun was a boy and teenager, they had spent a great deal of time together.

Usef said, "Suppose he asked you to marry him, which I don't know if he would, but, if he did, how would you be received by the Jewish community?"

Ruth said that she thought that need not be an issue. After all, they didn't live in biblical times and, today, there were many successful marriages between different faiths, for example, Catholics marry Protestants, blacks marry whites, and Arabs marry Europeans. She said, "Some of the pupils I teach are from a background of mixed race, but I do not know what Arun's opinion is. We have never discussed that situation. Besides, my mother is of Arab and Christian stock, and I am, therefore, so I am not purely Lebanese or Palestinian."

Ruth quickly changed the subject and asked her father how he was getting on with the new neighbour in Doctor Aserov's house.

Usef replied, "Not very well. He is most unfriendly. He says he will not let me herd the goats and sheep any more on his land. He says all this land belongs to the Jews and has been for thousands of years. To him, Palestinians are a scourge and should all be removed from Israel. He said that one day all this piece of land will be a Jewish settlement."

Usef said this attitude caused him concern, and if what his neighbour had said could happen, he could be deprived of his land and home. Ruth asked if they had heard from the doctor, but they said they had not, and were sorry that the doctor had moved. Ruth said she would not go call on the doctor; besides, she had to return to Jerusalem to be at the school the next day. She said a tearful farewell to her parents, at the same time making them a gift of money— Ruth was receiving a good income as a teacher. Usef and Letitia embraced her, and she then left to catch the bus at the bottom of the hill.

*   *   *

The months had passed, and it was now 1968. Ruth had not heard from Arun for some while, and this began to cause her concern. Supposing something had happened to him? However, his father would have let her know if anything was wrong. Perhaps he had become ill. Ruth could not get Arun out of her mind, and felt very low. Nevertheless, she had to remind herself that she had work to do and to concentrate on her teaching. Another month went past, and Ruth really began to think that something had happened to Arun. The waiting was extremely painful for her, not knowing if something had gone wrong. In her mind, she conjured up all sorts of disasters that could have happened, especially from terrorist attacks or bombings. She was not very happy, and felt very depressed. The news did not help matters. The whole world seemed embroiled with problems or violence, but, for all that, Israel was economically making headway, and the Jewish community was very industrious and pursued their lives with greater determination, despite the aggression and violence aimed at them.

Some Israelis had left the country because of the violence, and returned to the countries from where they originated; even those countries where their families had been persecuted during the war and brutally murdered. Now, they would not be subject to the fear and killings going on in Israel.

Ruth spent every day wondering what had happened to Arun and, sometimes, the idea came into her head that maybe, after all, there was too much difference in both their cultures.

Several more days came and went, and Ruth had returned to her apartment from the school. She was sitting quietly and still feeling lonely. Suddenly, she heard someone at the door. She got up, wondering who it could be— a neighbour, maybe. She cautiously opened the door and, with a look of amazement, realised that Arun was standing there. She motioned him into the room. He shut the door after him and, without a word, put his arms around Ruth and kissed her passionately. This was a complete surprise to her, but she responded with delight, and they held each other for some time. Arun was in his uniform. He let Ruth move away from him, then said how he had missed her and had thought about her, and was eager to see her again. She said she had been overcome with anxiety not hearing from him, and had been afraid something disastrous had befallen him. He explained to her the reasons why, but he did not want to upset Ruth by giving her any details. They sat and talked about his mother and father, and she told him of her visit to Usef and Letitia.

He said he would not be going to the Gaza Strip where he had been most of the time, which was giving them a lot of problems. There were lots of Israeli soldiers down there. His superiors had sent him back to a military position in Jerusalem, for which he was glad, because he would now be able to see more of Ruth. As the days passed, Arun kept his word and saw Ruth when he could and, in some of his free time, they went to cafés and restaurants and became closer.

* * *

The doctor had not seen Arun for some time and he, too, was always worried that something may happen to him. There was a lot of fighting between Israeli soldiers and Lebanese Palestinians in the south of that country, and fighting between groups in the north of Lebanon by refugees and religious political factions. In the south of Israel, the troubles were the result of the displacement by the Israeli government by force of the Palestinians from the West Bank. They had also built settlements on some parts of Palestinian occupied territory, and had to defend themselves from Syrian reprisals, having seized the Golan Heights. It was now a battlefield over the whole land and, although it had not affected him personally, Daniel had seen the results of such carnage in his work. The worst began to happen when suicide bombers, who liked to call themselves 'martyrs', began attacking civilians travelling on buses full of Jews, with disastrous consequences. A great number of these terrorists were from other Islamic countries. They tried to target numbers, which meant buses, cafés and shops, mainly owned by Jews and those Jews who travelled in buses. In quite a number of cases, many non-Israeli women and children were killed or wounded. The running battles between Arab youths were another headache for the army. They had to be constantly on the move to try to contain them. The youths, like their parents, had an axe to grind, as they were virtually incarcerated in refugee camps, and wanted their freedom to live a normal, peaceful life. Many of the occupants of the camps were just ordinary, hard-working, small farmers and stockholders who had been eking out a living on what was mainly harsh, rough land. Their ancestors had always lived like it and survived, but being deprived of freedom caused them to feel marginalised and deprived, and this led to anger and frustration, which caused them to take revenge.

*　*　*

Another year had passed, and nothing had changed very much in regard to the bloodshed and the inevitable tears that followed. Ruth and Arun had seen quite a lot of each other. He was now thirty-one years old, and she was twenty-five. They had been seeing each other for nearly a year. Arun, like his father, was quite liberal and modern in his thinking. Ruth knew that he was not an extrovert when it came to his religion. He had a deep sense of it, contrary to all the hatred that some Jewish groups spelt out against the Islamists and their followers. Arun was a compassionate person, although he did not show it. Deep inside, he could understand the anger that was tearing the country apart. Perhaps his attitude and understanding were the reasons he had come to no harm. He was a good man. He had inherited these attributes, no doubt, from his father. Also, he was fair and had calmed many a volatile situation by his diplomacy and reasoning, which was quite an achievement in those troubled times. He had told Ruth, the last time he had seen her, that he had something to tell her. He had arranged to see her on one of his days off, and said he would inform her which day. Ruth was wondering what he meant, and was excited about what he was going to tell her. She and Arun were deeply in love, so she was not quite sure what she expected him to say.

The day came and Arun arrived, again in uniform. Ruth opened the door to him and greeted him with the usual hug and kiss. They sat, and Ruth asked him if he would like something to drink.

He said, "No, thank you."

She asked him what he had to tell her, and he said, "Have you not noticed my new insignia here?" He pointed to his shoulders. "I have been promoted, and will have a headquarters in the city."

Ruth congratulated him, and said how pleased she was for him. Then he looked at Ruth with a serious expression, and asked, "Will you marry me?"

Ruth looked straight at him, and softly said, "Yes."

They embraced each other. Arun's face was now showing quite a lot of emotion, something he did not often do. Ruth was ecstatic. She was so happy that tears filled her eyes. Now she looked more beautiful than ever, and smiled. Together, they laughed and discussed how they would be married. Arun would take care of the details, he said, but there was one thing he had to do first. He had to get in touch with his father and mother and talk about their proposed marriage. He did not think that his parents would object, because he had previously informed them that he and Ruth had been meeting and socialising.

Arun made arrangements for Ruth and himself to pay a visit to Haifa to see the doctor and Druscilla. Being in a position of authority enabled him to do this, and they went by car to where his parents lived. They now lived in the town's Jewish area, near his work at the clinic. It had been some time since Daniel and Druscilla had seen Arun or Ruth. The last time she had seen the doctor was on a previous visit to her home when Arun had been south of the country near the Gaza area for quite a long time. When Arun arrived at the house with Ruth, Daniel was surprised, but greeted them affectionately. He called his wife, who was very happy to see them, and she, too, welcomed them. Daniel ushered them into the room, and Druscilla asked if they would like a drink or something to eat. Having made quite a long journey, Arun looked at Ruth and asked her if she would like something. She replied, "Yes."

Druscilla left the room to get the food and drink.

Arun then said to his father, "I have been promoted and given a post in Jerusalem, and I am the officer in charge. I only hope it is not going to be as violent as Gaza."

The doctor said how pleased he was for him. As his wife appeared with the food, he was eager to tell her the news, and she congratulated Arun and remarked that he deserved the promotion, as he was quite respected for his work in handling delicate situations.

After a while, having taken the food and drink, Arun said to of his parents, "I have something else to tell you."

He began by saying that, although he was now thirty-one years old, he had never had any interest in the women he had met, not even some who were serving with him in the army. He had always liked Ruth and, knowing her as playmates at her father's farm and in his teens, he knew that she was the only person he could fall in love with. At that moment, when Ruth reached out to put her hand in Arun's, his father and mother could see it was obvious they loved each other.

Then Arun said, "Ruth and I want to marry."

The doctor just looked at them and, for a moment, said nothing. Ruth felt very apprehensive, wondering what he would say. He then said, "You know, my son, I have never stood in your way at anything you wanted to do. Even though I did not like the idea of you joining the army after your conscript service, not because of your career, but that I might lose you through the violence." He then moved towards Ruth and Arun, put his arms around them and, with what seemed to be tears in his eyes, said, "Druscilla and I love you both very much. I feel that Ruth is part of our family. I helped to bring her into this world, and I am sure you will both be very happy."

Everyone seemed to talk at once, but having the acceptance from his father especially made them pleased and relaxed. Daniel asked Arun where he intended to get married, and he said it would possibly have to be a civil marriage, as this would not cause any hurt or even embarrassment among some Israelis who were anti everything concerning other nationalities. Besides, Ruth was not culturally involved with her own people, and her career as a teacher gave her the opportunity to be independent of other people's opinions. Daniel suggested that perhaps it would be better for them to get married in Haifa. They would not be living there, and Ruth would be accepted because no one would question her background and, of course, she had the assets of a beautiful woman to help her. They talked for a while on how to proceed with his father's suggestion, which he thought made good sense. The doctor said he would make some enquiries and consult the rabbi, who was quite an open-minded person and thought that many of his worshipers were bringing a lot of misery onto themselves with their unbending attitude. He also blamed ministers in the government who would not accept the word 'compromise', and, like Daniel, the rabbi had always thought that Partition would have been the best solution. Arun and Ruth were feeling happy and pleased

80

that his parents were agreeable to their marriage. Now they could look forward to their future. Arun said he must go back to Jerusalem to his post and take Ruth to her apartment. They embraced, and his parents and said farewell to them, then they left for the city.

*   *   *

The journey back was uneventful, which was good. Arun had patrolled some of the areas they passed through, and one of them was where he had met Ruth again. Arriving back in the city, Arun left Ruth at her home and made an arrangement to see her again, kissed her and left. He arrived at his post, and was told by an orderly that he had to speak urgently to one of the senior officers at the main headquarters. This caused Arun to wonder what the problem was. He got in touch, as he was requested, with the officer concerned, who told Arun that he would be taking a patrol the next morning to a village about thirty kilometres south of Jerusalem that was causing a lot of trouble to an Israeli settlement overlooking the village. It had been hit with mortar and rocket fire. This was something new. If it was Palestinians doing it from the village, they must be obtaining these weapons from outside sources. The next day, Arun drove with a platoon of armoured vehicles to the scene of the attack. When he arrived there, a small group of Israeli soldiers was already in position, discussing the situation with the officer of the unit. He learnt that two Israelis had been killed; also a woman and a child. Making enquiries with the settlers, he asked which direction the firing had come from. They said they could not give a precise area, as the attacks had come at night. The houses, being illuminated, were easy targets. Arun decided that he would drive with some of his patrol into the village to investigate the villagers and question them. Arriving with his vehicles, he drove into the village, and immediately ordered his soldiers to search the area. It appeared that most of the men had left, and only some women and children and a few old men were there. They questioned some of the old men, and they swore an oath that it was not the work of the people in the village. The people who had fired the mortars and rockets were from outside, and were unknown to them, and besides, it was night, and most of the villagers would be in the small cafés or at home. The old men said they never had a problem with the settlement. In fact, the shopkeepers did business with them, and they were sure these were raids organised by outside gangs trying to stir up trouble. So it had not been people from the village who had made the attacks.

Arun and his counterpart of the other groups of soldiers talked the situation over and came to the conclusion this could have been a hit and run tactic. This kind of assault had happened before, possibly seeing it as a way to put fear into the settlers. It was agreed that it was most unlikely that there would be any more incidents like it, at least for some time. Arun visited the settlers and gave his condolences to the families who had suffered, and told them to be diligent and take precautions, especially at night. With that, Arun and his platoon drove back to Jerusalem to his headquarters, leaving the other small platoon, which was stationed in the area to see the task completed.

*   *   *

On returning to his headquarters in Jerusalem, Arun got in touch with Ruth to see how she was, and said he would see her at the time and day he had arranged. He had not told her about the military operation he had just completed, in case it worried her. He said he had not had any news from his father regarding the wedding, but hoped that the rabbi had come up with a solution. He said the waiting was beginning to make him a little tense. The sooner they were married, the happier they would be.

A few days after meeting with Ruth, Arun got in touch with her and said he had heard from his parents. His father had seen the rabbi and had a long discussion with him. At first, he said the rabbi was a little cautious, but, as he had said to Daniel not very many days before, he hoped that everything would go according to plan. The rabbi brought up several points that may cause some problems. As Ruth was seen to be a Palestinian, he had to be careful not to offend some of the more orthodox sections, and thought it was out of the question to be married in the synagogue. They could only be married in a Registry Office by civil ceremony, and he would bless their union privately in the doctor's house. It was normal to worship in their homes. Jews are very family orientated, and regularly worship in private, or sometimes with friends and neighbours of the same religion. Arun knew this was so back in Russia, as there was no synagogue to worship in, so, being loyal to their religion, it was practised in the home. Also, the rabbi said Haifa was not only inhabited by Jews and Arabs. Other nationalities lived there, and he was sure it would be a very common occurrence for them to marry in a registry office.

Arun met with Ruth the next day, told her what his father had said, and asked if she agreed. Of course, he would not receive a negative answer! Ruth loved him so very much that she would do anything to make them happy. They kissed each other. Arun then said he would agree to what the rabbi had suggested. The rabbi knew how sensitive some Jews were to mixed marriages. It was especially so in the case of one of their kind marrying a Palestinian woman. Like Ruth, Arun was a modern thinker, and had adapted to the changing world. Technology had brought the universe closer. People travelled more and mixed in everyday actions, so it was becoming quite common for a mixed marriage to take place. They both said they would have to make an appointment for the ceremony, but, at the moment, Arun could not take time off from his duties. He would have to leave the organising to his parents.

*   *   *

Some days passed, and he received news from his father that he believed he had made the right arrangements to suit them. He gave them the date and time at the Registry Office. Daniel said he would also arrange with Arun's mother to have the reception at the house, and asked if he could let him know if this was convenient. Arun said he would see if it was possible to attend. Before replying, he would make sure he could be spared, and hoped that an emergency would not arise at his office. Arun got in touch by telephone, and said he would get in touch with his father right away. Things had gone a little quiet. So many things were happening around the world that it seemed as if Israel and the troubles had taken a back seat in world affairs, and Arun hoped it would last for a time.

The day came for their marriage. Ruth was feeling a little sad that her parents, Usef and Letitia, would not be there. It was not that she did not want them there. In a way, she really wanted to protect Arun and his family from any embarrassment. It made her feel uneasy that she was treating her parents like 'pariahs', and did not want to be like Usef's neighbour, who had been verbally abusive to him. Soon, Ruth recovered her thoughts and, with a smile, greeted Arun, who arrived to pick her up in his car. He was in civilian clothes and, as usual, looked equally handsome as he did in his uniform. They kissed each other, got in the car, and set off for Haifa. They talked about what they would do when they were married. Ruth said they would have to purchase another house, as Arun was in accommodation supplied by the military. He agreed that would be the right thing to do, and it would keep their lives more private. They were feeling content and a little nervous about what to expect when they arrived at his father's house.

On arriving, they were greeted by his parents and, in the house, were two or three people not known to Arun or Ruth. Daniel introduced them, saying they were some

84

associates from the clinic who would be witnesses for them at the wedding. Ruth and Arun acknowledged the group, who consisted of two married couples, and thanked them for being there. The time arrived, and Arun took Ruth's arm. She was looking very attractive, as usual, and they got into the car with his parents. They drove to the venue where the civil ceremony was to take place.

The wedding was performed quietly, with dignity and, on completion, the couple kissed, then thanked the administrator, the witnesses and his parents. Ruth and Arun felt happy and, looking very pleased, got in their cars and drove back to the doctor's house.

After they all arrived, Druscilla prepared a table with food and drink for them and the guests, who were the doctor's friends, who were arriving at the house. Among them was the rabbi, who was quite jovial and congratulated Ruth and Arun. Before anyone was seated, the rabbi announced that he would say prayers and bless the couple, saying that, afterwards, he was sure they would have a good life and hoped that their future would not be marred by the senseless violence that was ruining everyone's lives. Everything went according to plan, as Arun's father had organised. The doctor was happy for his son, and was glad that he was married to Ruth, for whom he had always had a liking. There was much talk and discussion amongst the group, but they talked of positive things and happenings, not wanting to put a damper on what was a special day. Time went very quickly. It was time to return to Jerusalem, and Arun, as a commander, could not be away from his duties too long. Saying farewell to their guests and his parents, Arun thanked the rabbi, who said goodbye and hoped that, in his position, nothing would happen to him or Ruth. Leaving the family behind, Ruth and Arun drove off with smiles on their faces, feeling deliriously happy.

They arrived safely back at Ruth's apartment and, when inside, embraced each other passionately. Arun had never stayed in the apartment at night before, but now it was quite in order to do so.

The next morning, he went to his headquarters to review any correspondence or orders that may have been given during the day he had been away. The situation had, in the past two or three weeks, been quiet and uneventful. There was too much going on in the rest of the world. Diplomatic activity was going on in some of the most turbulent countries, such as Africa. There was also upheaval in some European states; the main issue was the war in Vietnam, which was proving to be very costly, in lives and reputation, to the Americans, causing citizens in the Western world to protest, wanting an end to the ever-spiralling conflict.

*   *   *

It was now December 1968, and it was coming up to Christmas, so there were many people visiting Jerusalem. This was a delicate time for Israel, and particularly for Arun. The fear was that there may be a spate of bombings or other violence. It was not long before the calm was shattered. The news came through that some Arabs had attacked Israeli airliners in Athens and, in retaliation, the Israeli air force had attacked and destroyed thirteen Arab airliners in Beirut. This incident was happening not too far from Haifa, and retaliation, no doubt, would be taken by the Arabs. Now this situation was a worry, not only to Ruth, but also to Arun's family. If the southern Lebanon refugee camps with those that existed in Beirut took action, everything would descend into violence again. Nothing seemed to happen, and the year came to a close. Arun was pleased that he had not been called upon with his unit to any major incidents. Of course, there was always an existing problem. Almost daily, young Palestinians were venting their wrath by throwing missiles at patrols. This was becoming a kind of leisure activity for them. In the day, most of the men had some kind of work to do. A great number of Palestinians earned quite a fair income and supported themselves and their families working for Israelis. These people worked in factories, particularly in the horticultural industry, which was a booming business. Israel had a very good export market for their vegetables and fruit, which was a vital part of the economy. Despite all its troubles, Israel was thriving. It had a tourist industry, mainly in the south at places such as Eilat or Sinia, and many visitors pursuing their interest in the biblical aspects of the Holy Land, particularly Jerusalem.

Arun and Ruth were settling into their married life. Ruth still carried on with her teaching. They had both agreed to do this; otherwise, she would be sitting at home virtually doing nothing. Arun, in the meantime, had decided to search for a house. Ruth's apartment was a little too close to the Arab quarter. It would be much better to buy a house in the Jewish area of the city. After searching for a suitable property, he thought he had found a place that he believed would please Ruth. It was detached and large, with a garden. He was quite eager to tell Ruth of his discovery and show the house to her. They met with the agent who was handling the negotiations. When they arrived at the location and Ruth saw the house, she was quite excited. It was just as Arun had told her. The occupants were still living on the property. The agent knocked on the door and, as it opened, they could see a man who looked to be in his forties. He greeted them, saying he was expecting them. The man beckoned them in, motioned them to sit and, which was the usual etiquette, and offered them a drink. The agent started the conversation by introducing Ruth and Arun to the owner, saying he had agreed to Arun's terms and was pleased to sell him the house. Arun asked the man where he was going.

He replied, "I am moving to America. I have a manufacturing business in the town, which I sold to an Israeli. I have some relatives in America, but, unlike them, I came here from Europe before the Second World War started. In 1935, my family and I could see what was happening to Jews in Russia and Germany. Being single and young at the time, they chose to go to America, and I chose to make my future here in Israel, but, recently I have become disillusioned with the continuous violence, and cannot see a future for myself and my family here in Israel."

The agent looked at Arun and Ruth, and said the owner would be vacating the house in two weeks' time, then they could take possession. The man nodded in agreement. With that, the agent, Ruth and Arun got up, shook hands with the owner, and left. On the way back to their apartment, or their temporary home, for the time being, Ruth remarked to Arun that he had made a good choice buying the house. She said she would be pleased to live there, and was sure they would be happy.

* * *

Arun's mind had been occupied by the house. Now, he had to concentrate on his army commitments. It was moving up to the middle of 1969, and there was no let up in the troubles. The British, having a period of peaceful post-war existence, were suddenly confronted with a serious problem on their doorstep. At the same time, the Security Council had censured Israel for making a status change to Jerusalem. There was an uprising in Northern Ireland between the Catholics and Protestants. An age-old sore was being opened again. This had a parallel with the Palestinian troubles. They were both in the same position. Ireland— Eire— had, for half a century, tried to negotiate the return of the British-occupied territory. Both had the same purpose in mind. The Palestinians wanted their gardens back, and the Irish wanted their pastures back. Both were determined, and would fight to achieve this. Again, more blood and tears were to come in the future.

As agreed by the agent, the owner of the house had vacated it. Ruth and Arun moved into their new home, and soon settled down to their married life. It was nearly the end of the year, and everyone was hoping that the

Christmas period would pass peacefully. Arun resumed his duties with vigour. He was now in a relationship with the person he had always had in his mind to be with. Ruth had not seen her parents for some time, and suggested to Arun that she should visit them, as she felt they had been very much left out of what had been happening to them. He agreed with her, but was now a little apprehensive travelling to Haifa. There were sporadic outbreaks of violence all over the country, and he said she should be cautious. Ruth assured him that she would be all right and could handle any trouble. She had the benefit of being multi-lingual, and this could be her defence.

The next day, Ruth left for her parents' house near Haifa. The journey presented no problems. As a matter of fact, it was very quiet. Christmas had just passed, and all religious groups had celebrated the holiday period. Ruth arrived safely at her parents' house. Usef and Letitia were very happy to see her, eager to know how everything had gone with their wedding, and if she was happy. Ruth assured them that she was. She had always known Arun would be kind and considerate to her. Ruth asked her parents if she could stay overnight. She would go back the next day. Usef and Letitia said they would be very pleased for her to stay. Usef said that his neighbour was still very aggressive to him and Letitia, and they were still feeling insecure.

The next morning, Ruth set off to return to Jerusalem with an air of satisfaction. Driving back, she met a convoy of army vehicles and tanks. She was used to seeing such movements; after all, her husband was a commander of one of these units. Oblivious of what the movement was about, she continued her journey, but was soon to find out.

When she got back to Jerusalem and entered her new house, she heard on the radio that an emergency had occurred. Fighting had broken out on the Golan Heights—an area taken by the Israelis in the Six-Day War. Syria had clashed with Israelis, and reinforcements were being sent.

Ruth immediately got in touch with Arun's headquarters, but was told he was not there. He had taken his unit to reinforce the army unit already there. When travelling home, Ruth had had no idea that her husband had actually passed her en route. This really did worry her. If anything happened to him… That was not the only worry she had. She was pregnant, and had not told Arun.

Some days later, she received a message from him saying that the situation had been contained, and he hoped he would be back with his unit in a few days. Trouble was still the big issue. The Israelis were having more aggravation with the Egyptians. Their oil supplies were being sabotaged by them, so, having taken Sinia, the Israelis had built a pipeline from Eilat to eliminate this problem.

*　*　*

In Haifa, the doctor and his wife were following the actions daily, both by the Israelis and Arabs. They could see no end to all the atrocities that were being carried out in the name of democracy and, in a number of cases, religious bigotry. Everyone taking part in these actions seemed to think they were right and, at times, Daniel despaired. He was now approaching retirement age, and had not had very much leisure time. The clinic was like an assembly line of casualties, mainly Israeli soldiers wounded in the fighting in the Lebanon, and now from the Golan Heights. He had never seemed to have time to do the things he and Druscilla would have liked to do. He did have time off, but the furthest they went was to the coast to relax by the sea. It was one of the safest places to visit, as the Israeli navy patrolled the area. His ambition, when he and his family had arrived in Palestine, was to visit the holy places in Jerusalem relative to the Jewish faith and its architecture. He was optimistic that he would be able to do that one day when he had retired. He was getting tired of listening to the people in the government, some talking compromise, but most of them wanting more action. Did these people really think this was the way to bring peace to a nation that was making itself a target for all its enemies around the world? Bordering the State of Israel, in whatever direction you set your eyes, you were surrounded by enemies. Daniel's hopes and dreams as a young man with a young wife were being shattered every day. Although he was dedicated to his profession, which he always performed to a high standard, he was, at heart, very pessimistic of the future for Israel. The never-ending bad news did not bode well for its success as a peaceful nation. Most of the trouble that continually came its way was, to a certain extent, of their own making. Organisations like the United Nations, neutral states, and other countries that were being affected by the whole Middle East affair, had tried to seek a solution, and pleaded for both sides, Israeli and Palestinian, to cease the fighting and try to find a way for each to survive peacefully together. The onus was really upon the Israelis to compromise and listen, but this was not going to happen. The majority of the government was never going to accept any form of surrender. The fighting and retaliation had been going on for so many years that it had become a disease of hate. Even in response to minor disturbances by Palestinian groups, reprisals by the Israelis were brutally and excessively carried out. This tactic made the Palestinians and their supporters more violent and determined than ever. Different party followers, even in the Parliament, were not in agreement with each other, and the moderates had no sway in the military decisions that were taken. Still, life had to continue for the two parties. Some days it was good, especially for the Jewish communities who were much better off. None of them were incarcerated in refugee camps or suffering hardship and poverty. This was causing the Palestinians to rebel, especially those who had been deprived of their land and livelihood.

*   *   *

Arun had told Ruth he would soon be home, and he arrived with his unit back in Jerusalem at his headquarters. Ruth was so happy to see him and have him home again. Arun said there had been some very fierce clashes in the Golan Heights, but the Israelis had far superior forces, and the situation was soon calmed, with the Syrians retreating.

Arun had been at home and settled down when Ruth broke the news to him that she had something important to tell him. Eager to know what is was, he asked, "Is it good or bad?"

Ruth replied that it was good news, smiled at her husband, and said, "I am pregnant."

On hearing that, Arun jumped up, held Ruth and kissed her, expressing how happy he was, wondering if they would have a son or a daughter. Between them, they talked, wondering what they would call the baby if they had a boy. Ruth said she could easily have a girl. Both of them were very excited at the prospect of having a child. They were eager to tell his parents the good news. Arun could not wait to tell them. On hearing that his son was soon to have an heir, Daniel was delighted, and told Druscilla the news. This made the pair of them ecstatic, and a big smile came upon their faces. This was good news. It put new life into Daniel, and now he would put to one side what was going on in the country. Arun and his father kept in regular contact, and talked about the baby that was to arrive. Daniel was knowledgeable about childbirth, as Arun knew. He had helped with the birth of his wife, Ruth, and was eager to help and advise them. Daniel asked Ruth how long she had been pregnant. She told him four months, but said she did not show any obvious signs. Daniel took a much more positive view with his life. He was going to be a grandfather, and had something to look forward to. He fervently hoped that his grandchild would have a peaceful existence in the Promised Land.

Things may have changed for the doctor, but the upheaval of the fighting was still on everyone's mind. The Israeli prime minister had made an announcement that, if the Egyptians respected the ceasefire, Israel would no longer attack them. It was rather ironic that they, the Israelis, were appealing to their enemies to respect the agreed ceasefire between them, at the same time ignoring ceasefires requested from them to do the same with the Palestinians.

*　*　*

Ruth was still teaching at the college, and decided to do so until it was nearer the time to give birth. It was now into the middle of the year 1970, and Israel was being admonished by the Security Council for its actions in Lebanon. This was not good news for Ruth's parents, especially Letitia, who was from there and still had a number of relatives living in Lebanon. There had been disturbances amongst the different religions, whose followers were killing and fighting each other. Usef always thought it would not be safe to travel there. Even though it was not too far from where they lived to the border of Lebanon, they were consoled by the fact that, like Daniel, they were hoping to have a grandchild. That was something positive they could look forward to. Palestine and Israel were having a respite from serious violence, for the time being. The eyes of the world were turned to other matters, such as the trouble in Ireland. The odds were not the same for the militant groups who, like the Palestinians, were virtually fighting with small arms and home-made bombs, unlike the Israelis, who were heavily backed by the American government and the British, and had sophisticated weapons and a regular army. That, for the Palestinians, was the parallel between them and the Irish. Like them, they were fighting for the same cause. Fighting had broken out in Jordan. There were clashes between Palestinian guerrillas and the Jordanian army. This lasted for many days. Israel could once again take a deep breath that the conflict had not spilt onto their territory. Talks were going on with the United Nations, between the warring factions of Jordan, Palestine, Israel and Syria. An agreement was concluded between them, and it seemed a period of peace would be established. Amongst all the turmoil still erupting around the world, Ruth had left her teaching post and was preparing for the birth of her child. Fortunately, Arun had a quiet period, so was able to spend more time with her, and helped in whatever way he could. It would soon be coming up to Christmas 1970. Again, everyone would be praying that nothing would happen to blight this religious occasion. Ruth would give birth very soon. It was not many days before she contacted Arun at his headquarters, and said she should be taken to the hospital, as she knew the birth of the baby was imminent. He picked her up and went straight to the clinic. Being excited and nervous, Arun decided to wait at hospital. He had not long to wait. Within the hour, Ruth had given birth to a baby girl. A doctor approached him and told him the news. He could now go see his wife. Arun was smiling. So was Ruth. They had a lovely, healthy child, and were very pleased that the birth was without trauma, as Ruth had been born under difficult conditions. Now they would have to let his parents know. He was eager to tell them the good news. On hearing that Ruth had produced a girl, Daniel was a bit disappointed. He had hoped for a boy; nevertheless, he was happy for them, and remarked that, if the baby became like her mother, she would be a great asset to them, and also that he was anticipating the day he could see the baby.

* * *

It was now 1971. The world was still spinning in a cycle of madness. Israel was not making the news, but was not free from its problems. Its greatest supporter, the USA, was bogged down in the Vietnam War, seemingly without a hope of victory. Even though they had an overpowering superiority of armaments, they were in a no-win situation. Now, her citizens were getting tired of the bloodshed and casualties, brought to them by the news media, and they increasingly wished to see the fighting ended. Other disasters occurring around the world were natural happenings. The year progressed fairly peacefully on the Palestinian-Israeli front. The focus was now on Ireland and the atrocities that were happening to its people in the north. The cause of 'the troubles', as the conflict was euphemistically known, was not only about occupation; it was the hate shared by the two religious groups, the Catholics and the Protestants. How God became involved in this contest cannot be explained. Perhaps He had just been temporarily forgotten. Each party believed He was on their side.

Ruth was doing well with the baby girl. After much discussion, she and Arun had decided she should be called Deborah, which, in Hebrew, means 'a bee'. This was not merely a whim as, in the book of Judges in the Bible, Deborah was a prophetess who gave judgement on the children of Israel. They thought and hoped that Israel would once again be the 'Land of Milk and Honey' one day, and their daughter would have a peaceful, happy and productive life. Ruth was now beginning to take more interest in the Jewish religion, and would bring Deborah up in that faith. Of course, this would please Arun and his parents a great deal. The year passed fairly peacefully for Israel. The Irish troubles were making the news. Arun was now in a senior position in the army, and was a spokesman on 'military tactics', and spent some of his time in consultation with government ministers. He was now at the main defence headquarters, and had been elevated to the rank of colonel. He did, sometimes, have to do active service, to keep informed of the situations as they developed. Ruth felt more secure, and settled down to bringing up her daughter, Deborah.

*　*　*

It was now 1973. The year before had ended with some bad news. The Olympic Games were being held in

Munich, where Arab terrorists had attacked Israeli competitors, holding them hostage in their quarters. A battle had occurred with the guerrillas, and a number of Israelis were shot and killed.

Deborah was now nearly three years old, and was loved by her parents. Her grandparents had seen her two or three times in the last three years, but had not been able to visit them in Jerusalem. Ruth had driven up to Haifa, as disturbances had been fairly quiet in the villages and camps. Arun was now thirty-five years old, and Ruth was twenty-nine. Life had been quite good at this time, but the peace was about to be broken. War had reared its ugly head. On October 6, Israel was attacked by Egypt across the Suez Canal, which was still not open to shipping. Syria, too, had made an attack via the Golan Heights. By the end of October, a ceasefire had been agreed to, and a temporary peace was in place, for a time, at least. However, at the same time, Arabs had cut off oil supplies to Israel, making life difficult for them, demanding that Israel withdraw from the Palestinian-occupied territories. The thorn of occupation was getting deeper into the Israeli's skin, but the pain they were suffering was not going to make them surrender the land captured in the Six-day war in a hurry.

Arun was not spending much time with his wife and child. He was kept busy going from one location to another. At one end of the country was the Gaza Strip, which was a real challenge for the Israelis, as the people who occupied it were not easy to overcome, and were in possession of sophisticated weapons, which was causing great fear in the Jewish settlements outside that area. Ruth sometimes never knew where her husband was. Sometimes, he would be as far afield as the Lebanon. His brief was to monitor any situations taking place and report back to his superiors. This kept him on the move for long periods, but he did have some precious time to spend with Ruth and Deborah. Like Ruth, he loved his little girl who was now growing up and would soon be three years old. Being a teacher, her mother started her primary education at home, and was teaching her languages that she knew. Deborah was now in a Jewish family environment, and it was essential that she speak Arabic and English, besides Hebrew. This would be an asset to her in adult life.

The last year had passed without any major catastrophes. Trouble was mostly happening elsewhere, particularly in Ireland, where the IRA were making dangerous and unpredictable, random bombings and, as with Israel, the people who suffered were of the civilian population. They were also attacking targets in Britain, with the same results.

* * *

It was now into the year 1975. Israel was pulling its forces back from Suez. The canal would be open to shipping, but the Egyptians did not allow Israeli ships to use it. It seemed to be the same pattern of non-compromise. This 'tit for tat' hatred had now been going on for nearly thirty years, and, still, there was no end in sight.

Arun's father was now, sixty-five, coming up to retirement age, and looking forward to visiting Jerusalem while he and his wife were still able. Although he had very little time for pleasure, or to do the things he wanted to do, he had, nevertheless, had a fairly good life for the thirty years they had been in Israel. This was enhanced by the fact that they also had a grandchild whom they loved dearly. When retired, he would certainly be able to see more of her. The year came to a close, with more outbreaks of fighting in Lebanon, with the UN condemning Zionism for being racist, to which Israel reacted bitterly. The world was still in turmoil. Now, the African continent was having its problems, specifically for the same reasons as the Palestinians— freedom and independence from its colonial masters, in their case. Israel's economy was in a good state; the country was generally buoyant and surviving well, even with all its difficulties. It was another story for the Palestinians. Things were not the same. They had no economy, and not even representatives to speak for them. Most of them were either eking out a poor existence in the refugee camps in Lebanon, Jordan or their own country, surrounded by the extension of new Israeli settlements being built on the occupied territories. This was fuel on a furnace of wrath and hatred that the Palestinians and their supporters had for the occupiers.

Arun was kept busy with troop movements scattered over the different fighting zones, but was at home with Ruth every time he could be. He was seeing his daughter growing up as a bright, intelligent girl, like her mother. Deborah was now nearly five years old and attending a Jewish school. At the same time, to use her time and talents, Ruth returned to the international school where she had taught before, and was welcomed back. In some respects, it was beginning to quieten. The war in Vietnam was over, and diplomatic solutions had gone a long way to solving a number of the African disturbances. However, like the troubles in Ireland, things were getting progressively worse. Supporters of the left-wing Palestinian groups were carrying on with random terror strikes. The Israelis took swift action to one of these. Without any country's permission, they made a commando attack at Entebbe airfield to rescue one hundred Jews who had been held hostage, in a very successful operation. No one wanted to continually hear bad news. This was mostly aggravated by nations on the outside of the Palestinian-Israeli affair. Politicians in the newly formed EEC were advocating a Palestinians State. At the same time, the labour movement in Israel had been defeated, and the Likud party were in power, headed by Menachem Begin, who was, initially, a refugee from Poland and a devoted Zionist who had, in some people's view, been linked with Jewish terrorists in the past. It was obvious that the hard line he took was going to bode disaster for Palestine. He did make peace with the Egyptians, which calmed that situation, but the future was now more uncertain. Battles were being fought in the refugee camp in Lebanon between Christian forces. An agreement was later reached between all sides. The Syrian forces moved in as peacekeepers, into the middle of Beirut. Peace, once again, dared to raise its head, and the whole of Palestine and Israel were looking towards a non-violent Christmas and a chance to pray for an end to the senseless fighting and terror that was ruining their lives.

* * *

Arun was having more time off, with a lull in the disturbances. He, Ruth and Deborah would go to different venues, and see some of the more positive sides of life. They had plenty of friends in the Israeli community, and often entertained. Sometimes, Ruth and Deborah would visit the Arab quarter and buy fresh vegetables and fruit there. It was quite normal for them to do this. Nobody knew her real background in Jerusalem. As both she and Deborah were fluent in Arabic, it gave them the advantage of seeing the other side's day-by-day activities. She had no fear of anything happening to them, even though she dressed in mainly Western clothes. The 'East' side of Jerusalem was a 'no-go' area, and considered dangerous for non-Arabs. Ruth's experience in teaching different nationalities gave her the means to talk and make conversation with people easily. She did not find that she was intimidated. The Holy Land once again had a peaceful period at Christmas and into the New Year, now 1978. The only disaster that had spoilt the peace was the Israeli air force's attack on the refugee villages and camps in South Lebanon. Everyone was anxious, in this New Year, about what retaliation was to be meted out. They did not have long to wait. The PLO representative in London was shot dead. The Israeli forces made a massive attack and thrust into South Lebanon with huge amounts of tanks, troops and armour, advancing to the Litani River and obliterating Palestinian guerrilla bases. Again, this action only made things worse. It also affected Ruth, as Arun was amongst the tank troops there. This was the most worrying position she had been in for a long time.

Palestinian groups were now attacking the Israeli public by targeting buses carrying Jews, in some cases women and children, on the occupied West Bank. More terrorism came. A bomb exploded in the PLO headquarters in Beirut, killing one hundred people. Something had to give in, to stop this carnage that was destroying lives up and down the country. A meeting was held by the Americans at Camp David, and talks concluded with a signing of a Middle East peace treaty, to which the Israeli government agreed. Not long after, a ceasefire was agreed to, and a peace treaty signed by Egypt and Israel.

Usef and Letitia, Ruth's parents, were now really beginning to worry. They had told her that new houses for Israelis were being built all around them, and they were in fear of losing their house and land. Ruth found this very upsetting. She did not know what she should do. She had known that lots of Arab and Palestinians had lost their homes and livelihood by forceful means, that bulldozers had come and demolished them. This was done with the government's approval. The builders were supported and protected by the Israeli army if there was any resistance. Usef remembered what his Jewish neighbour had said, and this was happening. Usef asked Ruth if she could help him. This was a very difficult situation for her to be in, especially as her husband was a senior army officer. She promised her parents she would ask Arun for his opinion, while Arun was at home having a few days off with the lull in the fighting in Lebanon. After a lengthy discussion, they came to a decision that it would be wise for Usef and Letitia to sell their house and land before anything was forced upon them. The land they had was not enough to support many animals, since he could no longer rent his neighbour's land. If they were agreeable, it may save a lot of distress to them all. Ruth said she would help them to do this. It would be a great wrench for Letitia, whose family had lived there for a number of generations. Usef talked it over with her. It was a matter of life and death to them if they were to be forcefully removed. Where could they go? Letitia suggested the best option, if they did sell their house and land, would be to go back to Lebanon, where she had originally come from. She had plenty of relatives there, and they could start a new life together again.

*   *   *

It was coming to the end of another year. Israel was hoping again that the approaching Christmas period would be fairly peaceful. This was soon shattered by the explosion of a bomb in Jerusalem, then an Israeli attack on Palestinian guerrillas in South Lebanon. All this activity had the effect of more antagonism on both sides. Daniel and Druscilla were still in much the same situation as before. The fighting in the Lebanon was keeping him at the hospital with casualties from there, and hearing of the Jerusalem bombing caused him more concern. Some days, he got very depressed. This was often made worse, as he would never know what had happened to his parents. This made him sad. He was a sensitive man, and he despaired at what was going on in the land of Israel, the 'Promised Land' that promised nothing but never-ending fear and death. Some government ministers were looking for solutions, and others wanted more action against the Palestinians. The Israelis knew they had the upper hand. They had all the armaments and aircraft supplied by their biggest allies, the Americans, but there were a number of ministers in the government who were not happy with the actions that were being taken by the Israelis. Even members of the public who were not Zionist were open to compromise. Better, they said, to settle for a less demanding solution and live together in peace with the Palestinians by giving them their own autonomy and returning some of their occupied territory back to them. Of course, most of this rhetoric fell on deaf ears, but some demonstrations were taking place against the violence by some Israelis who had formed a peace movement.

101

After much debate about their future, Usef and Letitia summed up the situation in Lebanon. They thought it was becoming too dangerous to go back there. Besides, nothing had interfered with their lives so far. It was their house and land, and Usef was adamant that it would not be taken from them.

* * *

It was now the end of 1980, but there was no let up in the struggles in Ireland. The atrocities being meted out to each of the religious groups and civilians was horrendous. This, too, was being supported by outside intervention, as was the case with the Palestinians and Israelis. This made it more difficult for any ceasefires or political solution to be started or achieved, so the violence continued and, as in all acts of war, the people who suffered most were innocent civilians.

Arun and Ruth were inclined to agree with Usef, and said it would be unlikely that they would be dispossessed of their property. Whilst on his army patrols near the Lebanese border, Arun had sometimes been able to visit his parents, who were always delighted to see him. His father was now seventy years old. Often, he was disappointed that the troubles had not really let him achieve many of the things he would have wanted to do. It seemed his work as a doctor had never ended, with the day-to-day casualties being caused by what was, in his opinion, a senseless conflict. On his retirement, Druscilla said it would be better for them to move away from near the Lebanese border, which was continually a hotbed of trouble, and move to Jerusalem, to be nearer Arun and Ruth. This would make him happy. He would have all the leisure time he wanted. Daniel decided he would give his notice to the hospital as soon as he had found a house in Jerusalem. They told Arun and Ruth of their plans, who said they could stay with them until they had found a suitable property. After all, their house was quite large, and it would only be a temporary stay.

*   *   *

The next year was ushered in with only sporadic fighting in Israel, but Lebanon was still very volatile. Daniel had quit his position at the hospital, and they were very sorry to lose him. He had been a great asset to them. He had always made his medical profession his priority, and was proud that he had helped both Palestinians and Israelis, medically, to repair their broken lives. After a short time, Daniel and his wife said an emotional goodbye to their families and the rabbi, and set off for Jerusalem. Fortunately, having sold the house, they were not encumbered by a lot of possessions. It was some one hundred and forty kilometres to drive. They knew they would have to travel through villages and refugee camps that were aggressive and opposed to Israelis. They just had to hope that nothing would mar their journey. Being a man of experience with the issues around him, they had never dressed as Orthodox Jews. Druscilla and he had always worn Western clothes, ever since they had left Russia. This was the way they dressed, and they were not so conspicuous. Their fears came to nothing, and they arrived safely at Arun's house. The meeting was very emotional. It had been quite a long time since they had seen Ruth— at the wedding, in fact— and their granddaughter, who was now nearly twelve years old. They were thrilled to see her, and made quite a fuss of her. They were equally pleased to see Ruth, who was still a beautiful woman.

They settled into their life in Jerusalem quite quickly, and very soon found a house not too far away from Arun. Daniel could now pursue all the aspirations he had hoped to achieve. He became much more involved in his religion, and would soon be known and respected by his community. Of course, for the first time in years, they were close to their family. Everything was going well and, as with all Jewish families, they shared every occasion of celebration of their religion, and Daniel was a happy man. He put all the past behind him, and settled down to enjoy what was left of his life, together with Druscilla.

*   *   *

Arun was now forty-two years old, and Ruth was thirty-six. Both still retained their positions, Ruth at the college, and Arun in the army. Deborah was attending a Jewish school, and was progressing with her education; already, she spoke several languages, and would often go down to the Arab market with her mother and talk in Arabic with the traders as they bought produce from them.

Israel was prospering, and the world paid more attention to what was happening elsewhere. As for the rest of the world outside their borders, things were not satisfactory. Iraq, Syria and Iran were having their problems, making their lives uneasy. The Irish troubles were as bloody as ever, with no let up of shootings, bombings and revenge; a poisonous cocktail to swallow, resulting in more innocent victims being killed or maimed. In other parts of the world, nations were being thrown into chaos by revolutions and in-fighting. Generally, this wonderful world was turning out to be a disaster for many of its citizens.

The peace was soon to be broken again. A PLO representative to the EU Common Market organisation was shot and killed in Brussels. This action lighted the smouldering Palestinian touch-paper. It brought more suffering to Israel. They, in turn, did not wait for an answer or a reason from anyone to retaliate, and carried out a heavy attack in Lebanon on PLO guerrilla forces. This once-beautiful land was now, from the north to the south, one huge battlefield, with Beirut at its centre. Christians were fighting with Muslims; Syrians were fighting Lebanese. Also caught in the clashes were Americans, who had troops stationed there, as were French and UN forces. There were uprisings in the Gaza Strip and the West Bank.

The only good action that had come out of the year, so far, was that the Israelis had handed Sinai back to the Egyptians. More of the continuous 'tit for tat' violence was soon to follow. The Israeli ambassador in London was assassinated and, again, the Israeli air force bombed the Palestinian quarter of Beirut for two days, with devastating consequences, most of the area reduced to rubble. This was not the way to win friends and influence the Palestinians. A ceasefire had been agreed to, but was continually broken by both sides, more so by Israel, who had many weapons at their disposal. The president of the USA, Reagan, who was nearly the victim of an assassination himself, forced a ceasefire and offered a peace plan, which the Israelis rejected. Again, tragedy struck the Lebanese. Their leader was killed by a bomb in East Beirut. The PLO leader, Arafat, was having an audience with the pope in Rome. It was ironic that, whilst there, hundreds of Palestinians were massacred. Israeli troops had crossed the ceasefire line that had been established. They had also allowed Christian Phalangist militia to enter the Sabra refugee camp, with horrific results. This incursion by the Israelis brought worldwide condemnation and, with international pressure, Israel was made to make an inquiry into the massacre. The Israelis were forced to withdraw from Beirut, and more American troops were stationed there. In the midst of all these atrocities, the Aserov family, Usef, and Letitia were beginning to believe that there would be no end to the violence and hatred. How safe were they anywhere in Israel, and what would upset their lives next?

Only a month had lapsed. A huge explosion had just taken place at the HQ of the Israeli military base in Tyre in Lebanon. Usef was more than grateful that he had decided to remain where he was. How could they have survived in that devastated country? Ruth had something to be grateful for, as Arun had done a tour of duty there. Now, he was in Jerusalem. It seemed that an expectation of revenge on the suspects was about to happen. This did not occur. It was probably because the Israelis had been admonished for the massacre at the Beirut Refugee Camp and, with their ally, America, being displeased with their involvement, it made them wary to proceed with retaliation.

* * *

A period of calm once again descended. It was the month of December, and this was the time, according to the teaching of most faiths, for worship, contemplation, and a little brotherly love, if it still existed. The Christmas period passed without any serious disturbances, which was a miracle in itself. The New Year was ushered in with a repeat of the Beirut massacre, which was instrumental in the resignation of the Israeli defence minister.

Usef, who had enough on his mind, was now to have a much larger issue to confront. He had heard that, where his house and land were situated, was in the path of expansion of the Israeli settlements. His property was to be cleared for a new access road. This was the last thing he and Letitia wanted to hear. How could someone take his livelihood without his knowledge? He was very angry and upset. Now, what his unfriendly neighbour had said some years before was about to happen. Usef did not mention his problem to Ruth. He did not want to upset her, knowing her situation, and besides, Arun, his son-in-law, would have no authority over these projects; he was a military man. Usef approached the local government, made up of Palestinians. They confirmed that his land would be confiscated for a road to divide the Jewish settlement from the Palestinian village below. Apparently, settlers' houses were being continually targeted by snipers, which wounded some occupants. A road and barrier would be built and patrolled to deter the villagers, who had always protested that the shootings were carried out by outsiders. Usef was not satisfied with the answers he received, and went to the local Israeli authorities to put his case forward, but he was refused an audience. This disillusioned him immensely, and he decided he would make a stand against the takeover of his land. He was not the only Palestinian who would be affected. His adjoining Palestinian neighbours would also be deprived of their land. The villagers were not pleased with the proposed development. They waited to see what would happen. Nothing occurred immediately. Even the terror attacks had not been going on so frequently. The recent disaster in the Lebanon was still in Israeli minds. The calm was soon shattered, after the months without disturbance. Israel was again holding its breath with the bombing of the US Embassy in West Beirut. Very soon, the Israelis made an agreement with the Lebanon to withdraw its forces.

The Irish 'troubles' were still continuing, with terrible consequences. Using new tactics including vehicles loaded with high explosives; they unleashed devastating results to any innocent civilians who happened to be in the vicinity. Often, the IRA would give a warning when these acts would take place, unlike the Palestinians. Due to lack of time and their precise whereabouts, it was often too late to evacuate the public, with fatal results. The British mainland was being targeted frequently. How this would enable the Irish Republic to gain back its territory would not be taken lightly, and Northern Ireland suffered retaliation by the Protestants. Like the Palestinians, the burning issues, for generations, had been land and occupation. In Palestine's case, the Jewish solution was to open the country to large number of Jews from all over the world, which realised a majority for them, and resulted in a majority gaining power. This was the same as the Irish situation, who had had the numbers forced on them back in the seventeenth century, by the immigration of Scots and English colonists. Due to a potato famine, most of the Irish peasants emigrated and never returned; therefore, the numbers remaining had no power to resist.

* * *

The year was now nearly halfway through. Daniel

107

and Druscilla were enjoying their new, retired life, and had the pleasure of visiting and socialising with the family. He had now accepted that the past had to be put out of his mind, and that he had to enjoy what years were left for Druscilla and himself. Arun was still very busy, keeping control over any disturbances up and down the country. Ruth was still teaching and looking after Deborah, who was now approaching fourteen years old and taking an interest in her surroundings. She would sometimes go down to the Arab quarters to buy provisions. She liked the busyness of the market, and conversed with the traders. Ruth and Arun were not too keen for her to go by herself, but she assured them that nobody would harm her. Many citizens of Jerusalem— foreign and Jewish— purchased goods from the market. Deborah had even made friends with some of the young people she met. Where she lived, there were not any young people to be with. Even at school, she had not made any close friends.

Usef, in the meantime, was still a worried man. He expected, any day, for the bulldozers to come, but this didn't happen. Israel had made a peace deal with Lebanon, and a partial withdrawal. Only a few days after, an explosion in a Lebanese mosque killed many. Also, two US marines stationed in Lebanon with the International Peacekeeping Force were killed. Shortly after, the Israeli army withdrew from Beirut, and the US shelled artillery positions. It was complete chaos. Nobody seemed to know who was fighting whom. Then, by a miracle, a ceasefire was agreed to, and Israel had a new prime minister. Within days, a suicide bomber had killed two hundred and twenty-nine people, including fifty-eight French peacekeepers in Lebanon. In this period of time, Israel was having a calm existence. Again, Lebanon was going through this never-ending cycle of death and destruction in Tripoli. Arafat's supporters were battling it out with Syrian-backed rebels. Within days of this engagement, a car bomb in the Muslim area of Beirut exploded, killing a number of people. Arafat, with the supporter of four thousand guerrillas, left Tripoli by sea. Again, the last year had been a nightmare and a disaster for Lebanon.

* * *

The New Year started off much the same. The Lebanese Cabinet resigned after four days of bitter fighting between the Lebanese army and Shiite Muslims. US marines were removed to a ship anchored outside Beirut. British civilians were evacuated, and all, but one hundred US marines remained. Lebanon was now being abandoned, its demoralised population left to pick up the pieces. This tragedy of senseless killing and destruction was to be felt by the Israelis.

The reality came sooner, without warning. Daniel and Druscilla had been out, like many other citizens having just celebrated Easter. They were in Jerusalem, amongst the people casually walking around when, suddenly, a hand grenade was thrown into the crowd, causing injury to many of them. Daniel and Druscilla were unfortunate, and were badly injured. They were immediately rushed to hospital. Daniel's injuries were not life threatening, but Druscilla had been badly hurt and was seriously in danger of losing her life. Being a doctor, Daniel feared that she may not recover. Even though he was in great pain, Daniel would not leave her bedside. Every medic in the hospital was engaged in treating the wounded. They were doing their utmost to help Daniel's wife. The family were shocked at such an outrage. Ruth and Deborah rushed to the hospital to be with them. Arun had been given the news of the incident by the police and army personnel, who had immediately rushed to the scene. An Arab man was arrested and taken away by the police. Arun rushed to the hospital to see his mother, but, when he arrived, was devastated to learn that she had died from her injuries. Ruth and Deborah, together with Arun's father, were in shock, and were overcome with remorse. After all the family had done to find a safe haven and build a new life, it was a tragedy for all of them.

*   *   *

Arun was numbed by the death of his mother. He consoled his father, who was pale and distressed. Arun had encountered many deaths at scenes of violence, and the atrocities connected with them, but this was personal. Now, they, as a family, would have to start again, and face the world without the person they worshipped, who had still been a beautiful wife to his father. Arrangements were made with the rabbi for the funeral in keeping with the Jewish religion; the doctor was always very well respected, and his wife's funeral was attended by many friends and government ministers. After the internment, Daniel went to his house, and assured Arun and Ruth that he would manage by himself and wanted to mourn in private. Besides, he did have the help of servants. After a period of adjustment, Arun was back with his unit, and Ruth was teaching at the school. When he was at home, Arun was very quiet, and his smile seemed an effort. His conversation with his family was limited to just the normal greetings. He did not want to have any discussions. Trouble was still on the agenda for Israel. Individuals had been targeting buses again, and planting bombs in cafés frequented by Jews. The Palestinians were not very happy, either. Different groups, like Hamas and Hesbollah, were vying for power. A lot of in-fighting was going on, causing supporters of the groups to engage each other in violence. South Lebanon was still a flash point, with the Gaza Strip also in constant turmoil. Controlled by Israeli troops, it was one long battle between them and the Palestinians. Arun was still very upset by the death of his mother, Druscilla, which had been brought about, he believed, by Palestinians. Soon, he would leave Jerusalem and be sent to Gaza to take command of the army there, as he was now held the rank of colonel, but this, although a great credit for him, did not reconcile his sorrow. Ruth noticed how withdrawn he was, and did her utmost to comfort him. It was sad for her that some of her

110

country's citizens had been instrumental in bringing about this sadness and outrage.

Daniel had settled down, and tried to live a normal life again. He had lots of Jewish friends, who were very supportive of him. He was a little dismayed by the news that Arun had been posted in Gaza, considered to be one of the worst places where fighting and terrorism was taking place. The Palestinians were constantly firing home-made rockets into Israeli settlements, causing the army to take counter measures, which, inevitably, ended up in deaths, not only for the guerrillas, but also for the innocent Arab population, which included numbers of women and children.

Ruth and Deborah were worried that something could happen to Arun, just as it had to his mother, but, being in the army, it was his duty to obey any orders that were given to him. Some days later, he left for Gaza, with an emotional farewell. He still loved Ruth very much. He kissed Ruth and Deborah, and left. There was nothing Ruth could do, but to get on with life, concentrate on her career, and look after their child.

* * *

It was now 1984, a date with some sinister connotations and, sure enough, nothing had altered regarding the violence. Now, Arab buses were being sabotaged— by whom, it was not clear— making the situation more volatile than ever. In other parts of the world outside of Israel, other Arab sympathisers were helping the Palestinian guerrillas with arms supplies, and carrying out outrages on their behalf. America, Israel's friend and ally, was supplying more weapons and aircraft to them. The Palestinians were being supplied by their neighbours, and the Syrians by overseas sympathisers, the Libyans and Iran. This was causing a never-ending cycle of death and hate, which was not going to stop, even with the many proposals for peace settlements that were being put forward in Israel, which some members of the government were in favour of, but they did not have enough support to implement any realistic end to the conflict.

Meanwhile, the Jewish population carried on with their individual lives, and many had become prosperous. The infrastructure in Israel was continually being built up with many new commercial and leisure buildings, together with luxury venues in the coastal areas; the latter were being developed for tourism, which, it seemed, was not being curtailed by any threats of violence.

CHAPTER IV
The Disappearing Land

On the Palestinian side, the contrast was totally different. Most of its inhabitants were living in 'ghettos' or refugee camps, as they had been displaced from their land to make way for Israeli settlements. The camps had been established over a long period, and had now become townships and more permanent, with their own authorities, mostly self-appointed. The people, with the exception of a few rebels, just wanted stability and, if possible, their land returned to them. Ruth and Arun were in constant communication with each other. Ruth was always apprehensive, and feared something might befall him. She and Deborah were still busy, and did most things together. Deborah was still fascinated by the Arab quarter and made frequent visits there by herself, unknown to her parents. She was now nearly sixteen, and would soon have to decide her future. She was very bright and knowledgeable. With her language skills, it was obvious she would find a livelihood that would suit her. Her grandfather, Daniel, was very fond of her. He would take her to the places of interest in and around Jerusalem. It had been a little late in his life that he was able to do these things. He had hoped that his late wife, Druscilla, could share this with him.

Sometimes, he looked back to his days in Russia, and would have a deep feeling of remorse, wondering what had happened to his parents. He would blame himself for being selfish and felt cowardly, thinking he should have stood by the family and suffered whatever fate they had suffered.

Usef and Letitia, who were still very worried about what would happen to them, lived every day in fear of the bulldozers coming. All around him and his few Arab neighbours, more houses for Israelis were being built. He was watching every day, being enclosed by these houses, and was sure something would soon confirm his fears. Usef had not long to wait to find himself and Letitia in the nightmare that was about to begin. While he and his wife were sitting one day, having a meal, a knock was heard at his door. He got up to see who was there, and was confronted by two Israelis who had four armed soldiers with them. Usef asked them what they wanted. They told him that his land was to be taken over, together with his Arab neighbours' land. He would be given seven days to evacuate. Usef said he would require compensation for his property, or he would refuse to move. The party left, and Usef and Letitia were extremely upset that they were to be evicted from their house and land, which had been in the family possession for decades. He was, for the moment, at a loss as to what to do about it. He and Letitia talked it over. Having contact with the village below him, Usef said he would try to get the villagers on his side to try to stop the Israelis from taking his property.

* * *

The time elapsed and, on the appointed day, contractors turned up with moving equipment. With them were the armed vehicles carrying soldiers, who were also armed. This was a frightening situation for Usef and Letitia, who, by this time, were in tears. Usef tried to comfort Letitia. In the meantime, a group of villagers had arrived on the scene, and started shouting words of protest and harassed the contractors, calling them cowards and thieves. Employed by the contractors were some Arab workers, who came in for the worst abuse. Someone suggested stoning them.

Usef said to the group, "Don't start any violence; it will make the situation worse!"

However, a stone was thrown and hit one of the soldiers, who immediately fired his gun in the air. For a moment, this had the effect of calming the crowd that had gathered. This was only a temporary pause in the proceedings. The crowd began shouting and pushing, some trying to attack the Israeli contractors. This action caused the soldiers to enforce their authority. Being only a small force, their leader radioed his headquarters for more troops. In the meantime, more Palestinians had gathered, not all from the village, but from the surrounding area, which was also a threat to the Israelis. There was a lot of shouting and pushing, so the contractor's bulldozer could not start the work he was there to do. Another small contingent of soldiers in their vehicles appeared and, along with the soldiers already there, were forcing the crowd back. While this was going on, Usef seemed to have been absorbed into the crowd, but Letitia was still arguing and pleading with the soldiers. Suddenly, the Israeli officer in charge ordered the contractor to proceed with the work to start the road. No sooner had the machine pushed into the earth and rock, than all mayhem broke loose, and the crowd started throwing stones at the machines and soldiers. Letitia was defiant, and placed herself in front of the machine, standing her ground as it came close to her. Behind her was her home, and she was not going to see it brought down to a pile of rubble.

Above the noise, Usef's voice could be heard, calling her to come away. A shot rang out, and Letitia fell to the ground. Seeing what had happened, Usef rushed out of the crowd to her side. There was complete silence as he bent over her and tried to pick her up. Then he laid her down again, put his hands to his face, and wept. The crowd surrounded them, and some prayed and others remonstrated with the soldiers and demanded to know who had fired the shot. It was quite clear that the army had not, as the sound of the gunfire would have been heard there. It had to come from the Jewish settlement up the hill. The officer in charge of the army unit told the contractor to abandon the project.

The crowd had become silent, and began to disperse. Usef, with his neighbours, carried his wife back to his house. He was distraught with grief and numbed by tragedy. Before leaving the scene, the officer spoke to Usef and expressed his deep regret at the loss of his wife, and assured him that he would make enquiries among the Jewish community as to who was responsible for the shooting.

* * *

Along with the tragedy that had just happened in other areas, it was not going so well. Lebanon was still in a state of chaos, with in-fighting, political parties vying for power throughout the country, and the ongoing struggle in the south between Israeli troops and Palestinian refugees. In Israel, where there had been a period of peace, more car bombings and bus attacks were being made on the Jewish population. The Gaza Strip was still a tinderbox to the Israelis. Although their army was in occupation, they were having a lot of difficulty in keeping control. They were constantly under fire from snipers and suicide bombers. Jewish communities were still living there, and were being subjected to violence and harassment by the indigenous Palestinians, whose whole object was to remove them from Gaza.

Arun had received the news about what had happened at Usef's house, but as he had not made it public that Usef was his wife's father and Letitia her mother, he had to be very diplomatic about how he would deal with the situation. Ruth was totally shocked by what had happened, but knew that she could only grieve privately. She loved her husband so much that she would not betray him to her own family with the knowledge that she was a Palestinian. She could not attend her mother's funeral the following day, as it would be over by the time they got to

116

the Haifa area, where her father lived.

Daniel was very upset and shocked by what had happened, especially since he had helped Letitia with Ruth's birth. Arun and Ruth discussed what to do, and came to the decision that they would write a letter to Usef and tell him their feelings, and Arun would pursue who was responsible for Letitia's shooting, but they would keep the news of her grandmother's death from Deborah until she was older. Ruth was very upset by the loss of her mother. She decided she would give up her post at the college and spend more time at home. With the constant demands the army made on Arun, who seemed to be kept busy by the spontaneous attacks by the Palestinians on the Jewish communities, it seemed the right thing for her to do, and would give more time to her daughter Deborah. Also, it worried her to think of what might happen to her father, Usef, who now had a grave situation hanging over him, and knew that, sooner or later, he would lose his small piece of land and his home. It was disastrous enough to have lost his wife, and then the threat of eviction. It was not long before he was faced again with a dilemma. The contractors, who had temporarily ceased the work they had started, had returned to commence the work again. Usef was in a state of desperation and, before he could do anything, the officer in charge of the Israeli army unit that had been allocated to protect the contractors ordered them to start the work. No sooner had the bulldozer dug into the ground than a crowd had assembled. These were the same villagers as before. This time, they started to take action, picking up stones or anything that came to hand. The scene was looking as if it would become a battlefield. Again, the soldiers fired warning shots, but, this time, these were ignored by the crowd that gathered around the machines and fought with the contractor's employers. Again, shots were fired, this time into the crowd, and a woman and two men were wounded. This caused more mayhem, and the inevitable happened. Someone in the crowd fired a gun, and one of the soldiers fell to the ground. His fellow soldiers rushed to him, but it was obvious he was dead. They picked him up and put him in a vehicle. Again, the army sent for help and, within a short time, a larger number of troops arrived. In the meantime, arrests had been made by the army, and a number of the villagers were bundled into vehicles. Included amongst the prisoners was Usef, who had really done nothing but plead with them to let him keep his property. Again, it quietened down and, with the soldiers to guard them, the contractors recommenced working. Now, a number of Jewish settlers from the surrounding houses appeared on the scene and shouted abuse, taunting the villagers, who eventually returned to the village. No one knew what would happen to the prisoners, but it was certain they would be kept in custody for a time, and interrogated to find out who had killed the soldier.

*   *   *

Ruth and Arun, who were miles away in Jerusalem, were ignorant of the situation at this time, and knew nothing whatsoever of the incident. Some days later, a report appeared on Arun's desk at the HQ outlining what incidents had taken place and, as he read them, he noticed that another clash had occurred at Usef's house between the villagers and the army, with the loss of a soldier and wounding of three Arabs. On the list before him were the names of the suspects, and he saw Usef's name. In his position as colonel in the army, he had access to any information concerning acts of violence or terrorism, and was able to find out where Usef had been taken. He knew of the many Israeli defence posts near the Lebanon border, as Lebanon was still having many problems, both political and physical, with the Palestinians and Syrians. There were a number of prison camps under Israeli control. Arun was in a catch 22 situation. Should he try to get Usef released, or just leave the process to resolve itself? He knew, for Ruth's sake, that Usef had to be released, but where he would end up was beginning to become an issue. Finally, after much thought and words with Ruth, he made the decision to go to the Lebanese border to see what the military situation was, as a part of his duties. This would enable him to seek out Usef, and he would think of a way to resolve the case. Ruth agreed this could be the best way out for Usef. It was agreed that Ruth should stay at home and not tell Deborah anything, for the time being, just saying that her father had to go away on duty for a few days.

Arun duly arrived at the Lebanese border, which was still a hornet's nest, with Palestinian guerrillas in the south carrying out ferocious attacks on the Israeli defence positions. The army was still occupying the border region up to the river line. Enquiring amongst the various posts, Arun found out where Usef and his fellow prisoners were imprisoned. He told the officer in command of them that he would interview the suspects who had been involved in the episode that had taken place in the village at the outskirts of Haifa, and would see them the next day. Having an office at his disposal, he would interview them individually, with an officer and a soldier in attendance.

The next day, the prisoners were brought into the room, one at a time, in front of Arun. He questioned each one, asking who had fired the gun that killed the Israeli soldier. One after another— there were, altogether, nine prisoners, including Usef— all more or less gave the same story, saying that the person did not live in the village, but some said it was someone from the Jewish settlement who had intended to kill a Palestinian, and had killed one of his own kind by mistake. Usef, who was to be the seventh to be interviewed, was nervous and visibly frightened, not knowing what was in store for him. He approached Arun's desk and stood there looking quite blank. He did not utter a word. For a moment, Arun felt very uneasy. It seemed that, after so many years not seeing Arun, Usef had forgotten how he looked, as he was now very much older and in uniform. Arun looked at Usef, who was in a nervous state and physically shaking. Seeing him like that, before a word

119

was said, Arun called the officer to take him away. Arun himself was in a state of shock, as he was sure that Usef would have recognised him and, if he had, it may have embarrassed him in front of the guard. Fortunately, everything happened so quickly that a crisis was avoided. Arun now had to put his plan in order. He had given the order that the prisoners would be incarcerated for a period of twenty-eight days, and would be released if they undertook not to carry out violent or harmful actions when they were returned to the village; otherwise, they would be arrested again. Arun carried out some of his duties, visiting various Israeli security border posts, and had given the order to the officer who had attended his interrogations that the prisoner, Usef, would be collected and taken away for further questioning on a certain day. Having completed what he had set out to do, Arun returned to Jerusalem.

*   *   *

Returning home to Ruth was quite a relief, and he could tell her what had happened regarding Usef. Life was not going too well in Jerusalem; there were disturbances in the east of the city, and two suicide bombings in the western quarter, with the loss of a number of Israelis and some Arabs amongst them who had been dining at a restaurant. It was thought that the suicide bombers concerned came from the West Bank town of Nablis, which was virtually under siege and heavily guarded by Israeli troops and air cover, but the terrorists had the knowledge of how to avoid the strict security measures.

With the continuous occupation and the rapid building of new Jewish settlements, life for the poor Palestinian population of smallholders was daily seeing their land taken from them, with the government condoning it. They had no recourse to stop the theft of their land, and believed that they had had a right to the land before biblical times. This was not accepted by the Jewish population, who believed it was their land, ordained by God, which resulted in an impasse on both sides. Arun had a plan that would, perhaps, settle his problem with regards to the welfare of Usef, who, in Arun's mind, was a good man and was suffering a double blow with the loss of his wife, and now his land and home. This situation was out of Arun's jurisdiction. It was government policy to force occupation of the land on behalf of the settlers, who had now flooded into Palestine and Israel from all over the world.

Usef would not be the only one to suffer this legislation. Even though the United Nations and other countries had continually condemned the occupation and settlement, the Israeli government had ignored these complaints, and had carried on at a quicker pace. Usef's small piece of land, like that of his neighbours, would soon be covered with houses for Jewish settlers. As the house building progressed across the land of Palestine, they cast their shadows like a shroud over a corpse. Usef was still a prisoner with the others who had been arrested. Ruth was extremely worried that he may do something disastrous to himself. She urged Arun to do something soon to help him. It was not for Ruth's husband to get Usef's freedom, but, knowing from his wife that Usef still had relatives in the north of Lebanon, it was his intention to get his release by issuing an order to the post commander at the Lebanon border to the effect that Usef was to be released and taken across the border in a military vehicle, without obstruction, to the local Lebanese army post, who would then deliver him to his relatives in the north. There, he would be freed. Ruth would communicate with him in due course. Although, this would not be a happy end to Usef's troubles, as he had lost wife and his most valuable asset, his land and home, breaking a family tradition of occupancy down the centuries, but, unlike thousands of Muslim Palestinians, he was, at least, free. Arun received the news that his order had been carried out.

* * *

Time was eating the years away. It was now the decade of the nineties and, as was normal in these troubled times, the world was in disarray with civil wars in Africa and outrages and fighting in the Balkans. The United Nations was trying to keep the peace amongst many factions. A war was taking place on Israel's doorstep in Iraq. Once again, America and Britain were involved in Iraq. This was to prove a disaster for many years to come, and the catalyst for this war was mainly due to religious or tribal differences, but there was a strong belief amongst some that the real cause of the trouble was the occupation of Palestine, originally brought about by the Balfour declaration. In hindsight, he should have included a Palestinian state in his proposals, as well as Israel; this would have avoided the bloodshed and killing that was still ongoing. It would be, as long as the world depended on a barrel of oil: the real reason for the war in Iraq.

CHAPTER V
A Clash of Minds

Arun was now fifty, and Ruth was forty-four. Deborah was eighteen years old and studying at the Jewish school. Ruth was getting concerned by some of Deborah's habits. She knew she was fascinated by the Arab market. She would make an excuse to visit it, and always dressed in full Arab women's clothes. Ruth asked why she did this, and she said she felt safer and comfortable dressed like that. Her mother suspected that she could have other interests in the market, but, trying not to offend her by asking questions, was sure that Deborah would let her know of any matters that were bothering her. Then, one day, that's exactly what happened. In front of her mother and father, she declared that she was seeing an Arab boy of the same age as herself. His name was Ishmael. He was the son of the trader who Ruth had purchased provisions from many times. Ishmael, according to Deborah, was well educated, and had done some travelling as a student to other countries. He was highly intelligent and quite privileged. His parents were well off financially, and lived in a nice house. Arun and Ruth were a little taken aback by Deborah's admission, and suspected that she may have fallen in love with Ishmael. Nothing was said for a time. It was not easy for either of them to interfere with Deborah's plans, whatever they might be, as they themselves were not conventional in their own relationship, as Palestinian and Jew.

Daniel was now eighty years old, and still in good

health, having got over the shock of his beloved Druscilla's untimely death. He had pulled himself together and carried on with his life. He was fortunate to have many friends and a son- and daughter-in-law. The Jewish community around him was friendly and helpful, and he still had lots of interests, like architecture and biblical places, to study. He was still quite bright, and lived life to the full. One thing that never left his mind was the ongoing violence still happening, mainly in the cities, the West Bank and Gaza. Politicians, both Israeli and Palestinian, had come and gone without bringing about a solution for the reconciliation of the country's situation, these politicians and prime ministers, most of whom were dead or, in some cases, assassinated. It left, in their place, a government consisting mainly of introverted and inflexible politicians who gave their ear more to the 'Orthodox' rather than the compassionate Jewish communities, who would be prepared to make a compromise with the Palestinians over their grievances, if it meant a Palestinian State alongside that of Israel.

Daniel was always hopeful that this would be achieved in his lifetime, and Israel would once again be peaceful and tolerant. However, all his hopes were soon dashed by more violence in the Lebanon, Gaza and the West Bank, and in his own city of Jerusalem, much of the trouble being brought about by different Palestinian and Arab terrorist groups who could not agree amongst themselves. This was causing more misery for their people. Generally, Israel was prospering, and its economy was buoyant. Tourism was popular, and the coastal towns of Haifa and Tel Aviv, along with many of the smaller coastal towns, were attracting tourists. As the violence in the West Bank and the Gaza Strip was sporadically occurring, the coastal area was reasonably peaceful as the Israeli navy constantly patrolled the shores. Many Palestinians had secured work in the hotels and catering businesses, which were mostly Jewish owned, unlike their fellow Palestinians who, on the other hand, were in a poor economic state.

Many on the West Bank lived in poor conditions in country areas, and, having had most of their land taken from them, could not support their families and, in many cases, depended on food handouts from a number of charities.

Ruth, who was now feeling very sad at the disaster that had happened to her father, Usef, was now more worried about Deborah. Arun was not too happy, either. They asked themselves what was going on in her mind. Deborah had no plans to take a position in some kind of career. Like her mother, she was highly intelligent, and had her good looks. It would not be a problem for her to secure employment. They were soon to receive another shock. Deborah told them she was going to change her name from 'Deborah', which she thought was too Jewish. Besides, Ishmael, her boyfriend, did not care for it. She said they had both agreed her new name would be Hagar. All this was very upsetting to Arun and Ruth, who had always had the idea that Deborah would settle down to a successful career, and possibly marry an Israeli boy. There was really nothing they could do about it, as Deborah was of age, and had every right to determine her own future.

*   *   *

The days ahead were looking very gloomy for the family. Ruth had been in touch with her father Usef, who was still living with an aunt and uncle of Letitia's, his late wife, in a small village outside Tripoli in the north of Lebanon. There, he was safe and away from the trouble of the south. However, Usef was not happy. He was still very upset and shocked by the loss of his wife and smallholding. At times, he became very depressed, according to his late wife's relatives, who were afraid he might do something drastic.

The troubles were piling up on Ruth. Arun, too, was having a hard time controlling outbursts of random attacks on Jewish settlements up and down the country. Now, his daughter was allying herself with the Palestinians, who were perceived as the enemy. Ruth told Arun that it would be kinder not to let his father know just yet what problems they were having at the moment. Ruth and Arun visited Daniel quite often, and it would be difficult for them to contain the knowledge they had of Deborah's intentions.

After one of her frequent visits to the Arab quarter's market, Deborah, who now wanted to be called Hagar, asked her mother if she could introduce Ishmael to the family. She said she had been introduced to Ishmael's. Ruth put the question to Arun when he arrived home, after being away for a few days on duties. When Arun heard what Ruth had to say, he went a little pale, turned away, and said nothing for a minute or two. Turning to face Ruth again, he said, quite sharply, "No, it would not be a good idea. Besides, I am not in favour of Deborah associating with an Arab boy, irrespective of what his parents' position is." Then he added curtly, "I do not want to hear anything more about it."

This came as a shock to Deborah. Now calling herself 'Hagar', she was, for the first time in her life, being turned down by her father. Perhaps she could not understand her father's attitude; maybe he was viewing Ishmael as a potential enemy, but he could also be upset by the fact that an Arab had been instrumental in the death of his mother; this was an emotion that could only be understood by Arun.

*　*　*

While the Aserovs were trying to solve their personal problems, in the outside world, it was as chaotic as ever. Terror and killings were normal daily events in places like Pakistan, Indonesia, Iraq, and Ireland. Africa, too, was in a state of unrest in the Congo Somalia. A lot of the troubles were of the same mould: politics, religious bigotry, and land grabbing. It had become a daily happening for many of the citizens of these places. In some cases, these disturbances were caused by the Western world's appetite

126

for oil, which was considered, by some leaders of the Western democracies, more valuable than the human lives whose country the oil happened to be in, in reality, making excuses that they were bringing democracy and freedom to them. However, to most of the populations of the Eastern world, democracy was a Western notion. All they wanted was to follow their own customs and religion, without interference from outside forces, and to have a peaceful life and stability.

*　*　*

Events now unfolded to make a dramatic change to the Aserov family. Hagar had absorbed herself into the Arab culture, always dressing in Arab-style clothes and attending a mosque with Ishmael. She sometimes did not return home for days, which was a great worry to her family. She told her parents, when she did come home, that they should not worry about her. She never stayed at Ishmael's house, but at his sisters' house, who lived away from Ishmael in part of the eastern sector of Jerusalem. For a while, Hagar, as she now liked to be called, spent less time at home. When she did go shopping with her mother, it looked a little odd with Ruth wearing Western clothes and Hagar in Arab dress, but she did not wear any face covering. It was not an unusual sight, as many Arab students were seen talking and in the company of people in different clothes, especially people who were of the business class.

Deep down, Hagar would feel, at times, that she had deserted her family, and would sometimes embrace her mother and say how much she still loved her. To her father, she had a much cooler attitude, but would still approach him at times and kiss his cheek. This situation went on for some time, then the final shock came, out of the blue. Hagar announced, one day when she came home, that she and Ishmael had decided to get married. This was not what Arun and Ruth wanted to happen. All the time, they had

127

thought that their Deborah was just playing a kind of game, and she would come to her senses one day. Arun and Ruth were speechless and, at first, it looked like Deborah— her parents still called her that— was still playing a game with them. However, that was not on Deborah's mind. She again repeated what she had said was true. She was going to marry Ishmael. Questions were asked by her parents, such as, "Does Ishmael's father agree with your marrying?"

Deborah replied that they had not told him yet. Arun said he would not agree to her marrying the Arab boy. They were still young, and perhaps he was just using her to swell his ego. Ruth had little to say. Her eyes swelling up with tears, Deborah then dropped a bombshell by saying that the Jews hated the Arabs and were responsible for all the misery that had overtaken Israel and the Arab world, and that she did not want to be a part of the Jewish community. Arun got the impression that she was being indoctrinated by her boyfriend, Ishmael, and told Deborah that she should come to her senses and realise the mistake she was making. Ruth still said nothing, but was emotionally in turmoil. She had, in all their married life, never had arguments of any kind. Then, suddenly, out of character— he had always shown tolerance, like his father, Daniel— Arun told Deborah that if she married Ishmael, it would cause the end of their relationship, and he would have nothing more to do with her. Ruth intervened at this point, and said sternly to Deborah, "Your father does not mean what he says."

With that, Arun looked stern and retorted, "Yes, I do mean exactly what I have said."

With that, he left the room. Hagar stood looking pale and visibly annoyed with her father. She then put her arms around her mother and hugged and kissed her, then ran out of the house in tears.

She went to the market, where she knew Ishmael would be. Then, when they met, he could see that Hagar, as he now called her, had been crying. Hagar told him what her father had said when she told him that she was going to

128

marry him. This made Ishmael very angry. He got the idea into his head that Hagar's family did not like the marriage of their daughter to an Arab, and he took this as contempt. Deborah would now wonder what Ishmael's parents would say, when they had the courage to ask them.

* * *

Some days later, Deborah was still staying with Ishmael's sisters, and, between them, they decided to ask Ishmael's parents for their permission to marry. They went to Ishmael's family home. Deborah had been there before, a number of times, but only to his parents' house as a friend, and not a lover. Everything was going well for the couple, having a social type of meeting and talking of mundane things that were happening around them. It now came to the moment for Ishmael to announce his intentions. Rather nervously, and in a shaky voice, he asked his father, whose name was Ahmed, if he would allow him to marry Hagar. For a while, everything went quiet.

Ahmed then asked, "Why do you want to marry Hagar?"

Ishmael replied that they loved each other.

Ahmed said to his son, in front of Deborah, "Do you realise she is a Jew?"

Ishmael said that he knew that from the beginning of their relationship, saying that, in this day and age, it was quite normal and acceptable for different ethnic groups to marry without any problems.

Ahmed then asked Hagar if they had asked permission from her parents. For a moment, she said nothing. Ishmael looked at her and wondered what she would say.

Hagar then stood straight, looked at Ahmed, and said, "My parents, particularly my father, do not like the idea of me marrying an Arab."

Ahmed's face took on a look of surprise, and he looked a little perplexed. Again, he questioned Hagar, asking her what else her father had said.

She replied, "He will disown me."

Ahmed's once calm and pleasant manner now turned tense and unsmiling, and he said that they had both better come to their senses, forget the whole idea of marriage, and go their own ways in the world. From now on, they should not see each other. At that, Deborah left, with tears in her eyes. Ishmael was told by his father to stay where he was.

Deborah had only one recourse. She would now have to go back to her mother and father's home, and suffer the consequences of her emotions.

Ruth was delighted to have her daughter at home again. Arun thought his talk had turned the tables, and convinced Deborah she had made an emotional mistake and would soon get over her recent setback. For a while, the atmosphere in the Aserov house was a little subdued. Deborah was not very forthcoming in any conversation. She still went to the market, but only to see Ishmael's sisters, who were keeping her visit secretly from Ishmael's parents.

*   *   *

Daniel still had no idea of the situation at Arun's house. Ruth made a visit to him, which was a routine she had now and again, to make sure he was being cared for by the servant he had, who was of mixed Arab race. She found him not to be the bright, cheerful man he had been recently; he seemed to have deteriorated since her last visit. It was obvious, according to Ruth, that he was not well. She got in touch with Arun, and told him that she was very worried about his father. Arun, who was at his HQ, left and went to his father's house. Ruth had contacted him from there, and waited for him to arrive. When he arrived, he was shocked and upset to see his father in the condition Ruth had described. After asking his father one or two questions on how he felt, Daniel replied, in a soft voice, that he did not know. He said he just felt unwell. Arun and Ruth decided that he should be taken to the clinic immediately. Rather than take him themselves, they phoned for an ambulance, which came quite quickly. Ruth and Arun both went to the clinic to make sure that Daniel would be attended to; the doctors there would probably tell them what the matter was with him. One of the younger doctors who had worked with Daniel in the past in Haifa recognised him, and assured Arun that he would be well taken care of. This was another upset for Arun and Ruth who, with Deborah, were not having a very good life. Worse was to come. While Arun's father was in the clinic, Deborah was planning her next move. Unknown to her parents, she had written a letter asking Ishmael to meet her after dark at his sisters' house, and to bring any money he was able to obtain of his own. She would do the same. She had saved a sum of money, given to her, at times, by her parents. As she didn't have a career, she did not have a great amount to take with her. In her letter to Ishmael, she had arranged that they should meet at his sisters' home on a certain day. All this had to be carried out without the knowledge of his parents. His sisters would know what Hagar was planning, and they had vowed to keep their elopement a secret in the name of Allah. They had to also make certain that no man or relatives would be present when they met at his sisters' house. Ishmael very soon got in touch with Hagar and, two days later, they would meet as arranged, after dark, at his sisters' house.

*   *   *

When the time came, Ishmael arrived first, and made sure that only his two sisters were there. Deborah had made the excuse to her parents that she was going out for a while to have a walk. Before doing so, she went up to her mother and told her how much she loved them, and kissed her. She approached her father and kissed him on both cheeks. Neither Arun nor Ruth was suspicious of her actions. With the condition of Daniel on their minds, they were diverted from thinking about what Deborah may or may not be doing. She went, as arranged, to the eastern sector of the city, dressed in Arab attire, which she had not abandoned. She found the coast was clear when she arrived, and immediately hugged and kissed Ishmael. Hagar asked him how he had managed to leave his house. He said he had told his father, Ahmed, that he was going to a café to drink tea with his friends. This seemed to be acceptable to Ahmed. Not wanting to waste time, Ishmael and Hagar said a tearful farewell to Ishmael's sisters, reminding them not to divulge what they were doing. Neither Ishmael nor Hagar had decided where they would go, but they would not stay in Jerusalem, as they would be easily found. Ishmael, who had travelled around quite a lot, suggested they could either go to Ramallah or to Hebron. Neither place was too far away from Jerusalem, although both places were towns with a record for violence and protest. Ishmael thought these places had many displaced Palestinians living there, and it would be hard to find them.

Once out of the eastern sector of Jerusalem, they took a taxi driven by an Arab, and asked him to drive them to Hebron, telling him they had missed the late bus back and that they lived there and wanted to get back home. The driver agreed on a price with them, then set off. That night, neither Ishmael nor Hagar's parents were too worried, knowing that, at their ages, they had no jurisdiction over them, and thought they would turn up in due course. Ruth and Arun had bad news from the clinic, in that his father was deteriorating, and they were advised to come as soon as they could. When they arrived at the clinic, they could see that Daniel, who was now eighty-two years old, was dying, and Arun could only look on, knowing that this was the end for his father, who had always loved and considered him all his life. Arun and Ruth could not hold back their tears. The most important person in their lives was about to be taken away from them; a man of great compassion and feeling who, all his working life, had dedicated himself to helping his fellow men, irrespective of their nationality, while his own kind were destroying lives. For all the years he had lived in Israel, he had prided himself by saving many a man who was in favour of compromise and justice. He would not live to see an end to the bloodshed and violence that, for decades, had caused fear and uncertainty in his 'Promised Land'. Daniel, who was still conscious, but visibly very frail and weak, held his son's hand while Ruth looked on. It was only to be a few moments before Daniel breathed his last breath, then everything was still and silent. A clinic doctor approached the bed and closed Daniel's eyes. Arun and Ruth knew that this was the end, and they would now have to arrange the funeral. Feeling utterly sad, both of them returned to their house, and would now have to break the news to Hagar.

When they got home, of course, she was not there, but, being overcome with grief for the loss of his father, Arun did not pay much attention to the absence of his daughter. It seemed a disaster that, at this very time of their grief, an emergency should arise. A bomb had exploded in Jerusalem's west sector, and caused a loss of life to both Jews and Palestinians, who were in a shopping area. Some tourists had also been killed, and a soldier who had been patrolling in the area. Arun was summoned immediately to go the scene. On arrival, he encountered the sight of bodies and blood everywhere around. The ambulance services were there, as were many people helping the wounded, with a number of police and soldiers. Arun, in his position as a senior officer, was given details from the military and police on what had caused the explosion. It was clear a car bomb had been detonated, but who was responsible was not known at that time. It was believed to be the work of the group called Hamas, an organisation that had taken over the monopoly from other more moderate parties, and their policy was the eradication of the Jewish State.

* * *

Arun, who had witnessed many bloody incidents,

showed no emotion. Having just lost his father seemed to have numbed his feelings. He knew that he was up against a very powerful force that had influence on the Palestinian population. Also, they were helped and armed by outside supporters from the Islamic countries around them. Arun had no means of really finding the perpetrators of these acts of violence. The only way the military could find out where the Hamas supporters or leaders would be was by intelligence and surveillance. The new tactic was to find and destroy the leaders by air. The means of this was to target hideouts of the Hamas commanders, which were mainly in the built-up, Arab-occupied towns or refugee camps. The Israeli air force carried out these attacks with great precision, but, unfortunately, many civilians were killed in the process, including many women and children. This did not stop the terrorist attacks, but made the overall situation worse. Many efforts were made by various nations for peace talks to take place, with a stop to these acts committed by both the Israelis and the Palestinians, but, as usual, they fell on deaf ears. The story was still the same. No one was prepared to listen.

*　*　*

Returning home, Arun was about to receive more disturbing news. Ruth had found a note in Hagar's bedroom, saying that she and Ishmael had left Jerusalem together and that she was going to live with him somewhere; the actual location, she did not divulge, but she said she loved them both, and she was sure she would be all right.

This was a cruel blow for Arun at a time when he had just lost his father, and now his daughter. It seemed doubly disastrous, as now he was the only survivor in his family. Without Ruth, he would have no one. Ruth had always been very supportive of him, and loved him. They still had a great deal of affection for each other, and this would be the bond that would see them through all their recent setbacks. Now, they had the sad ceremony of burying Daniel. Arun would arrange this with the rabbi, who was as shocked and upset by his death as Arun and Ruth. The rabbi had become a great friend and comfort to Daniel in his retirement. They were both caring and compassionate people, and had very much the same mindset on the future of the State of Israel.

After his father's funeral had taken place, Arun now had to think about what their future was going to be. Without Deborah, Ruth would now find her life a little empty. Although he was nearing retirement age, Arun was not prepared to think about that. He thought he still had enough strength and, being in good health, he could still carry out his military duties for a few years yet and, like many Israelis, he hoped that terrorism would be defeated one day, either by force or the better solution of some kind of mutual agreement between the Israelis and Palestinians. This was a very bleak hope. Troubles were still breaking out, especially in Gaza and the West Bank. Ruth had not had any communication from Deborah, and was constantly worried about what had happened to her, if she was all right, and if anything had befallen her.

* * *

In the meantime, Hagar and Ishmael had reached Hebron, and had found a place to stay temporarily, in the centre of town, in a small bed and breakfast place kept by an Arab, who turned out to be quite inquisitive, and asked them many questions about their status, if they were married and what Ishmael did for a living. They had to be very careful how they replied. It could make the man suspicious. Ishmael, being wiser in worldly affairs, told the man he had a position in the town with a lawyer, and would be starting in two or three days' time, and hoped they could stay for that length of time. The Arab seemed satisfied by Ishmael's answer, and said they could stay. Ishmael was more than happy that he had influenced him. Hagar thought he had done very well to cover up what was really going on between them.

The next day, they both went out into the town, and Hagar was surprised that they were actually staying close to a collection of houses in the middle of mainly Arab dwellings. Another surprise to them was the large number of armed soldiers in various places, and standing in doorways. The reason they were there could be in case of any trouble, but it looked more that they were mainly around the Jewish houses, keeping watch over them in case of any violence they might encounter. Ishmael did not like the area, and told Hagar that they must find somewhere out of the area, further out of the town. If they were stopped by the soldiers and asked for identity, they would be in trouble. Hagar agreed that, as her father was in the army, she would easily be discovered, as, no doubt, he had been in touch with army personnel to look out for her.

That night, they paid the Arab for their stay, telling him they had found another place nearer where he was going to work. With that, they picked up the few belongings they had, and departed as quickly as they could under the cover of darkness. They made their way along the back streets of the town, trying to avoid any brightly lighted areas. A sense of panic was beginning to come over Hagar. She kept close to Ishmael. The streets were becoming darker, and the roads were rough and dusty. She asked Ishmael how much further they were going. He said they were nearly at the part of town that was mainly occupied by refugees, and it would be difficult to find them there.

Hagar said insistently, "We must find somewhere to sleep. I am very tired with all the walking we have done."

Ishmael told her not to worry, as he would find them a place. The only lights were from the houses and one or two cafés, and it was not easy to distinguish what the houses were. He was sure that, if they went to one of the cafés and asked the proprietor, he would tell them where they could stay for the night. Seeking out the most brightly

136

lighted place, Ishmael told Hagar to wait outside while he enquired. After a few minutes, he came out, then suddenly went back inside, returning before long with something in his hands. Ishmael said, "I knew you would be hungry, like me, so I have purchased some food for us to eat."

Before attempting to eat the food, Hagar asked Ishmael if he had found a place for them for the night. He said the man in the café told him he could try to ask at a house a few yards up the road. A widow there sometimes took in lodgers to boost her income, but he did not know what she charged.

Ishmael and Hagar still had some money that they had brought with them originally, and were hoping it would see them through the immediate future, at least until Ishmael could find work. It was not very easy to find the house. Once away from the café lights, it became much darker. Ishmael looked for the house they thought fit the description the café owner had given. After searching for a while, they came to the door of the house and knocked, not knowing what sort of reception they would receive. A woman in her late fifties answered the door, and asked what they wanted. Ishmael said that the man in the café had told him that she might give them accommodation for the night. At first, the woman looked at them and did not say anything. Then she asked them who they were and what they were doing there. She remarked that they looked quite young, and was curious to know why they had come to this area. Ishmael had to think very quickly, and came up with the excuse that he had some relatives in the area, but, not having visited them before, he was unsure where they lived, and had decided to wait until the morning to find them, when he could find his way around. The woman was convinced he was telling the truth. She asked them to come in, but, first, they would have to pay her. Ishmael and Hagar entered the house, which looked quite bare, with very little furniture or appliances, but the bedrooms were tidy and the beds looked comfortable. There were two rooms, and the woman asked which room they would like.

Hagar said they would have the larger room. Ishmael asked the woman if she had any family. She said she did have, at one time, but two years before, there had been a lot of trouble. A number of local youths had started a riot with some Israeli soldiers who had come into the camp and arrested some Palestinian men, saying they were terrorists. This had caused a lot of tension. Then numbers of men and women had come onto the street, including her husband and son. The youths were stoning the soldiers and their vehicles, who responded with tear gas, but that did not stop them. Someone fired shots and wounded three soldiers. The other soldiers immediately opened fire on the crowd, which killed her husband and son, and now she was left to make a living by herself. Ishmael said how sorry he was to hear of her loss, and assured her that, one day, 'we will have a free Palestine'. Hagar, in the meantime, had not said anything. This was the first time she had met anyone who had suffered at the hands of the army. The woman then asked if they would like something to eat. They replied that they had had some food at the café. Ishmael and Hagar were happy that they had, at least, secured a place to sleep and, in the morning, they would have a look around to see if there was a flat or house that they could rent. Until he got work, their money would help them. Hagar was wondering what her parents were thinking.

Ruth and Arun thought that it would not be long before they saw their daughter again, but when, was the question.

* * *

The next morning, Ishmael and Hagar left the house where they had slept, and thanked the woman for her kindness in accommodating them. When they got outside, they were shocked to see what was there. Further up the road were houses and buildings in ruins, and many of the houses standing were riddled with bullet holes. This did not look very optimistic for them. How could they find a place here, even if it was temporary? There were children playing amongst the rubble, and a few goats clambering about, too. Several groups of men and a few women were talking with each other. Numbers of older men were sitting outside the bullet-ridden homes and drinking tea.

Hagar said to Ishmael, "What can we do? There does not seem to be a building that is habitable."

Ishmael said he would ask some of the men who were sitting if they knew of any place they could rent. One of the old men said they may be able to rent a property, but not in that part of the town. Ishmael asked him where he suggested they should look.

He replied, "You have to go further to the outside of this area."

He said he knew that some concrete blocks of flats had been built two or three years ago; they had been trouble-free. Ishmael thanked him and said goodbye, and they set off up the road again. As they went along the street, the houses did not look damaged by Israeli army incursions. They felt more optimistic; now, they had to find somewhere to live. Once again, Ishmael decided to ask another old man if he knew if there were any lawyers or agents here. The old man asked why he wanted to know. It seemed, to Ishmael, that everyone wanted to know his business, and were very suspicious of him. Ishmael assured him that all he was looking for was a place her could rent.

The old man looked at Hagar, and asked, "Are you married?"

Hagar said, "Yes."

The old man smiled again. He then came up with the news that there was a lawyer in the place, and gave them the directions. Again, Ishmael thanked him, shook hands, and set about finding the lawyer's place of business. He soon came across a dwelling that he assumed was his office. It looked like quite a professional place. This gave Ishmael more confidence in getting information.

* * *

The lawyer was a man in his forties, quite stout and big. Welcoming Ishmael to his office, he asked him to sit, and shouted to someone in the house. A woman appeared, and the lawyer asked her to bring them some coffee. Again, Ishmael was asked what services he required, and why. Ishmael said that he and his wife were looking for a flat to rent. To Ishmael's surprise, he asked how long they wanted it for.

"Yes, I own a number of flats," he said. "Would you want it for a long term or short term?"

Ishmael had to think fast again, and said at least six months. The lawyer said he had a block of six flats just up the road, and that they may be lucky, as he had one vacant. The man who had been living there before had been taken away by the police. He had been accused of terrorism, along with a number of others. Also, his house had been full of weapons, which had made him vulnerable. His wife had left the flat, as she could not pay the rent. Ishmael was again questioned, and asked if he had had any problems with the military.

Ishmael replied, "No, never." Besides, he thought there were better ways of solving disputes than by force. "How much is the rent for the flat? That is, if you will let us have it."

The lawyer told him how much per month. Ishmael, again thinking quickly, calculated how much money he and Hagar had, and was pleased to discover it was more than enough for their rent. The lawyer closed the deal after Ishmael had handed over a month's rent in advance. With a smile on their faces, Ishmael and Hagar went out of the office, following the lawyer, who was taking them to the flat.

On arrival at the building, they saw it was concrete and looked like it could do with some attention. In the surrounding area were four more of these buildings, which all appeared to be occupied, by the fact that washing and bedclothes were hung out on the balconies. Ishmael's flat was on the second floor, and looked over an area of squalor, but it was far enough away not to interfere with them. Entering the flats with the lawyer, up the concrete stairs, he stopped at the one that Ishmael had taken. On entering, it was much the same as the number of dwellings in the poorer areas. Ishmael and Hagar had always lived in modern houses, so how would they adapt to this situation and lifestyle? Having accepted the keys from the lawyer, they shook hands, saying goodbye to him. Then the lawyer went on his way. Ishmael and Hagar, for a moment, were silent, taking in the scene before them.

Ishmael, always being optimistic, remarked to Hagar, "Never mind, I will soon get the flat in order."

At the same time, he embraced Hagar, who looked at him and smiled.

First, Ishmael said, he would have to find a bed and blankets. Also, they needed cooking utensils and food. In a few days, he would be able to make the flat more comfortable. He said he would go out and see if he could find these things, and would have to spend some of the money they had, and hoped he would later obtain work to earn some money to cover their future expenses. With that, he kissed Hagar and told her to lock the door after him, and he hoped he would be back soon with the goods. While he was gone, Hagar had time to think, and immediately wondered how her mother was and how she would be feeling. She knew her dramatic departure would be a shock to her father and mother. Thinking about them made her a little depressed, but she had done what she had done of her own free will. At the same time, she was very much in love with Ishmael, and that gave her cause to be more cheerful. More than three hours has passed, and there was no sign of Ishmael's return. Hagar was beginning to be a little nervous, thinking that something had happened to him, but her fears were soon dismissed as a knock at the door told her that Ishmael had returned. Eager to know what he had purchased, she looked at the things he had brought with him. He had food, kitchen utensils, and two blankets. She

141

asked Ishmael if he had found a bed, and he replied that he was unable to find one. It seemed that they would have to sleep on the floor on the blankets for a night, but he said, before they would have to do that, he would make another attempt to get a bed, saying that there must be somewhere to buy one. Kissing Hagar and telling her again to lock the door, he left. As he went down the stairs in the flat, he met a man coming up.

The man asked Ishmael, "Are you our new neighbour?"

Ishmael replied, "Yes, we have only moved in today."

He asked the man if he knew where he could purchase a bed.

The man said, "Yes, but you have to go nearer the town, or the market."

Ishmael said he really did not have the time. He had already searched the area for a second-hand shop, and was unable to find anything.

With that, the man asked, "Is the bed just for you?"

Ishmael replied, "No, it's for my wife and myself. Why don't I introduce you to her, as we will be neighbours for some time to come?"

The man was elderly and, like a lot of older Palestinians, dressed in traditional Arab clothes, unlike Ishmael, who preferred Western style clothes. Going back to the flat with him, Hagar answered the door, and was surprised to see Ishmael with another man. Ishmael introduced the man, who said his name was Mohamed, and that he lived in the flat next to them. The man acknowledged Hagar, and then remarked to Ishmael how privileged he was to have such a beautiful wife, which pleased Ishmael, and he smiled at Hagar.

The old man said, "Did you say that, without a bed, you will have to sleep on the floor? You cannot do that. It would be most uncomfortable. I have a spare bed you can have. I live with my son and his wife, who are in their fifties, and their two sons are now married and live in the main town, where they work. I would be pleased to let you have the bed, but you will have to come with me, as I'm afraid it would be too much for me to carry. Perhaps your wife could assist you in carrying it?"

To this, Hagar replied, "Yes, I will help. I am quite strong."

They all went into the man's flat, who first introduced Ishmael and Hagar, giving their names to his family, who, at first sight would have no idea that Hagar was Jewish, especially the way she was dressed. They would never know unless she told them, but she was clever enough not to give them any ideas, as she spoke in Arabic all the time, although she would sometimes speak Hebrew, when shopping in the town of Hebron, with Jewish shopkeepers. Having entered the flat, the old man showed them into a room that was empty, except for a bed. Much to their surprise, it was big and well made. With a smile on his face, Ishmael asked the old man if he was sure he could spare it, and what he wanted in money for it. He had another pleasant surprise.

The old man said, "Nothing."

He was glad to help them as neighbours, and asked if there was anything else they wanted help with.

Ishmael said, "I think we have what we want for the time being."

With that, he and Hagar took hold of the bed, which was quite heavy. Nevertheless, they managed to juggle it through the door of the old man's flat towards their own, which was opposite, struggling to get it into their flat. At last, they succeeded. Ishmael went back to the door while an exhausted Hagar had a rest on the bed, and thanked the old man, who had been looking on to see how they were doing. The man turned away, waving.

Ishmael closed the door and went over to Hagar, who was still sitting on the bed. He put his arms around her and kissed her. They could not believe how fortunate they were to have a kind neighbour, and also a bed. That night, they cooked themselves the first meal on the bottled gas stove that the previous occupant had left, and settled down to a good night's rest. Before they slept, Ishmael said that, first thing in the morning, he must find a job, but would discuss it in the morning, as he was too tired to talk about it right then.

Waking up in the morning after a good night's sleep, they both felt refreshed, and were in a very optimistic mood. During the breakfast that Hagar had cooked, Ishmael said, "There are a number of jobs I can do; I can account, which I did for my father; I can repair motor vehicles, and I studied for a degree in law, which, unfortunately I can no longer finance, without the help of my father, who, I am afraid, does not want me now, and I'm sure he will disown me because of what we have done." Then, holding Hagar, he added, "I love you so very much that I would give up anything." He also said that, although he would not dress too Western, he would wear the same as most of his young friends, so that he would not look too much out of place. With that, he said, "I will go now, but I don't know exactly when I will be back."

Giving Hagar one last kiss, he then left.

* * *

While Ishmael and Hagar were sorting out their lives, many more were being lost through all the violence, still as cruel as ever, in the important places like Gaza, Jerusalem, Hebron and Ramallah. Almost daily, incidents and clashes with the Israeli military took place. With all these acts of atrocity, it would end up with the whole country shedding more Israeli and Palestinian blood, and many countries looked on, as they had their own troubles to think about, and were not interested in the situation in Palestine. Still, no one listened to the many attempts that were made to have some kind of ceasefire and a peace deal. As before, neither side was flexible enough to come to a compromise.

Whilst Hagar was home alone, lots of thoughts

came into her head, mostly about her mother and father. Ruth and Arun's lives had been put in turmoil with the events that had recently befallen them, especially with Arun, who had lost his father and mother. It was a cruel blow for him to be parted from his daughter, too, even though the latter was his own doing. Ruth felt the pain, too, with the loss of her mother, Letitia, and her father, Usef, losing his beloved house and farm. Even that was only the beginning. Now she had lost her first and only child. Sometimes, she thought that if she had given birth to another child, a boy, or even another girl, she would have had someone to comfort her. This was a very depressing time for Ruth and Arun, but, as always, they still had and loved each other. Ruth had not been in touch with her father, and wondered if he was all right, as he had not contacted her for some time.

CHAPTER VI
The Reality

Ishmael had returned home, looking quite pleased with himself.

Hagar asked him, "How did you manage? Did you get any work?"

Holding her, Ishmael said, "Yes, yes. I was really taken aback by the Arab who owns the garage, if you remember? It was just out of the town, where there are plenty of vehicles and lots of cars and buses moving up and down the road. He said he could do with another mechanic, as one of his employees was a fairly old man, and he needed someone younger to take his place, as the older man was not strong enough for a lot of the tasks he had to do. He said he wasn't sacking him, and that he was leaving of his own free will. He said he could find much easier work where he lives."

Ishmael then said that they had agreed on a wage, and this was quite good, on the condition that he could do his work well; if not, he would have to let him go. However, Ishmael was bright and adaptable. Having driven a car for some time to his studies at home in Jerusalem, he had quite a lot of mechanical experience, and believed he could do the work. The Arab had said he could start on the next Monday, which was in four days' time. All this put new life into both of them, and they talked about what they would do when they had saved enough money.

Everything seemed to be going well and, for a time they, forgot the situation they were in. Time seemed to go very quickly. Hagar settled down very well, and got on with all her neighbours, who were not only Palestinians. Some were from Jordan originally, and some of their wives were Egyptian. Everyone seemed to co-operate with each other.

Ishmael had started his job, and had proven that he was capable of doing his work. His only gripe was that all the cars and vehicles were old. He would like to be able to work on new cars. The old cars were time-consuming; most were in a bad state and grimy and a number were literally falling apart. Also, it was a dirty job, together with the smell from welding, which they did a lot of, but the wages were good and he did not intend to stay there for too many years, anyway. He always kept a lookout for a better job. This one would suffice, for the time being.

Although it was a far cry from what Hagar was accustomed to, it was not too bad. There was a bakery shop, and even a small medical centre that was financed by an outside charity. The surroundings, like many of these refugee camps, were pretty squalid. They did not have the services of the town population, but water was available, and most other services were created by the camp occupants to give themselves some kind of dignity and, in many ways, they were self-supporting. Some of the more fortunate had managed to get work in the main town. These were mainly young to middle-aged men and women. Most of the others were their older parents and other old men who had lost their land and homes. Even this did not make them lose their pride, and this could be seen on their faces.

* * *

Time was passing quite quickly, and a glimmer of hope appeared in world affairs. The Irish had made a compromise towards a peace settlement, and agreed to lay down their arms on both sides. There were agreements reached in other parts of the world, and a ceasefire was made amongst the fighting factions in the Balkans, but there was still little hope of any peace settlement in Israel. There were still day-to-day incidents occurring between Palestinians and Syrians against the Jews, as in both warring parties. The parties who would be open to a compromise were always overruled by the zealots on both sides, who were supported, on the Palestinian side, by 'Hamas' and their entourage, while Israel had a mighty military force.

Arun had been fully occupied with his duties, but, like Ruth, Hagar was a big worry for them. They had no communication with her, either by telephone or letter. Ruth was to have yet another shock. Her relatives in the Lebanon had been in touch with her, telling her with regret that her father, Usef, was dead. They had found him in his room when they had gone to waken him in the morning. He seemed not to have suffered any problem with his health, but they thought he had become very introverted and silent for quite some time, and Ruth's aunt believed he died of a broken heart. With the loss of his wife, Letitia, and then his land, he could not face life. Ruth was shocked at the news, and told Arun that she must go say goodbye to her father, and he would now have to help her to get a pass across the border from Israel into the Lebanon, which was always heavily guarded. Arun said he had the power to give her a pass, but she would have to travel under her maiden name. This would not cause any embarrassment to either of them. Duly processing a pass for Ruth, she kissed Arun and left, saying she would let him know of the time she would return.

Fortunately, Ruth had no problem getting to her aunt's house in the Lebanon. It had been many years since she had seen her relatives. It was quite a surprise for them, seeing Ruth after such a long time, but they were taken aback by her good looks, even at her age of fifty-plus years.

Arrangements had been made for the burial of her father, which would take place the next day. Ruth was visibly upset by the loss of her father. She had always known him as a kind, compassionate man, and wished that the circumstances that had kept them apart had never happened. Now, it was all too late. She had to go back to her husband and home, and would be wondering what disaster was looming in the near future. She arrived back home after her father's burial, feeling very low and depressed; it was a great comfort to be back with her husband, Arun.

* * *

As time passed without any serious setbacks, Israel was having longer periods of peaceful existence, which were still always very fragile, as violence and bombings could break out at any time.

Hagar and Ishmael were still making a home for themselves, helped by the money he received from his work at the garage. He was getting quite used to getting up and going to work and, in between, attending prayers at a small mosque that had been built by the refugees. Hagar would sometimes attend with him at the women's division. They had now been in the flat for five months, and Hagar was about to make an announcement to Ishmael. He arrived home later in the evening. She greeted him, putting her arms around him, saying she had something to tell him. Eager to know, he asked what she had to say. With a big smile, she told him that she thought she was pregnant.

Ishmael jumped up and down with joy, and asked, "Will it be a girl or a boy?"

Hagar said she did not know, but hoped they could have a son. Ishmael said it would be wonderful for them, and declared he would work longer to get some more money, as they would need it.

As the days went past, Hagar began to show her pregnancy, and could not keep it a secret. Ishmael met the woman from the flat near them, where her father-in-law had given them the bed, the next day on his way to work. He gave her the good news. She said that she hoped he would be the proud father of a boy, and that it would take

149

after him. Ishmael thanked her for the compliment, and went on his way to work. Hagar was in a quandary about whether to get in touch with her parents now, or wait until the baby was born. She would discuss this with Ishmael when he returned to the flat. That night, they talked of what would be the best thing to do. Hagar was keen to get in touch with her parents, saying it might reconcile them, but Ishmael said it would be better to wait for the baby to be born, as it could be either a boy or a girl. This meant they had some time to wait before the birth was due, but it would be the thing to do. Hagar accepted his advice. They again hugged each other to confirm their feelings.

* * *

For some time, the little world around them had been peaceful, and Ishmael and Hagar prepared themselves for the happy event to come. It was now nearing the time for Hagar to give birth. Although it was just eight months, it was obvious by her size that she could have the child any day. Soon, Hagar was having bouts of panic and feeling very exhausted. Three days later, she told Ishmael that she knew she would give birth soon. She told Ishmael to go to the clinic and ask if anyone would help her, as she was in a certain amount of pain and would need help. Ishmael rushed off to the clinic, and soon reappeared with a young woman who could not be any older than Hagar. She introduced herself, said she was competent in midwifery, and immediately gave Hagar an inspection. She remarked that the birth was imminent, and asked if Ishmael could ask the neighbour if she would help. With that, he went next door and knocked. The woman answered the door. Ishmael excitedly told her that they needed some help, and asked if she would be kind enough to do that. The woman was more than willing and, together, they returned to his flat and found that Hagar had gone into the last stages of labour. The midwife asked the woman if she would help by getting water and towels, which she did. It was not too long, with a certain amount of screaming and crying, before Hagar gave birth to a fine, healthy boy. There were smiles all around, the midwife saying how well Hagar had done, and without any complications. Ishmael, of course, could not disguise his joy, being the proud father of a son. The woman from the opposite flat, having assisted with the birth, told Hagar that she could ask her any time she needed any help in the future, as she would be pleased to give it. With that, the woman and the midwife left, wishing Ishmael and Hagar future happiness with their new son.

A few days went past, and Ishmael brought up the subject of a name for the boy. Having gone through a list of names, they both agreed the boy would be called Ibrahim, a good name for an Arab boy. Hagar settled down once more to her domestic life and looking after their son, whilst Ishmael carried on with his work at the petrol station and garage.

* * *

Trouble was still brewing for the Palestinians. More and more settlements were being built for the Jewish community, and more of the Palestinians were losing their land and homes. All this action was still being taken, in spite of United Nation's directives. Also, more Jews were being allowed in to swell the Israeli population, therefore increasing more tension and hatred from the Palestinians and their supporters. Outbursts of violence were occurring daily on the West Bank and the Gaza Strip, with periodic clashes on the Golan Heights.

The reality of the situation was now beginning to have an effect on Ishmael and Hagar's lives. Hebron had been having a respite since the last outburst at a café by a suicide bomber. This respite was again to be broken. Where Ishmael was working, there had been an explosion in a small shopping area, with loss of life to a number of shoppers. Immediately, the army was at the scene, and started closing off the area. A cordon was put around the adjacent streets, and it shut off the garage and the properties around it. This looked quite bad for Ishmael and the others working there. Before they could do anything, they were suddenly surrounded by soldiers who started asking questions. The soldiers believed that someone from the refugee camps was implicated in this act of terror, and had forbidden anyone to move until they had been questioned. Ishmael panicked at the thought of being arrested with some of the others, as he could be held prisoner. What would happen to Hagar if he was taken away? His heart was beating fast, when, with the garage owner, they were all lined up. Some of the workers were not young, and it made Ishmael stand out more. They were all asked for their identity. Ishmael's heart sank even lower as the soldier looked at his pass. Much to his surprise, he gave it back to him, doing the same to the other workers. The soldiers left, and everyone was relieved that it was over. The only problem was that the garage was shut off from the town, and business was likely to be affected. This was going to be another worry for Ishmael. With no business, he could be without a job. A number of the refugee camp occupants were customers, which helped, but the main work came from the town side to the garage. It was imperative that Ishmael earn more money, now that he had a wife and son to keep. When he arrived back home that night, he told Hagar what had happened to him, and described how he had felt when being questioned, together with the prospect of losing his job. What would he do if that happened? For the next few months, Ishmael carried on with his daily routine of work. He told Hagar ruefully that he could soon lose his job at the garage, as business was slow. Their new son, Ibrahim, was keeping them occupied and doing well. Hagar suggested that, in the event of him losing his job, why did he not look for some other work, to which he replied that it would not be easy and, in any case, it was uncertain for how long the area would be closed to the town. Ishmael had an idea. He said he would approach the lawyer who owned the flat. Perhaps he would take him on as a clerk or bookkeeper. It would be worth a try. He could only say that he did not require anyone.

*   *   *

The next day, he asked his employer if he could leave for a short period, as he had something to attend to. The owner of the garage said he could, and told him he may have to leave, as they were running out of clients. Ishmael thanked him and set off for the lawyer's office. He did not know how he would be received, and was a little apprehensive. Entering the office, he greeted the lawyer, who acknowledged him, and then asked why he had come. Hesitating, Ishmael asked if he had a vacancy for a clerk or bookkeeper.

"Why do you ask?" the man replied.

Ishmael said that he would prefer to do clerical work, as he had been well educated and felt that the work he was doing at present was a waste of his talent. The lawyer was not a young man, and did all his own work, which, for him, was quite time absorbing.

The lawyer said nothing for a moment, then said, "I might consider you, but I want time to think about it."

Ishmael did not mention to him that he had been presented with a son by his wife, in case it could be seen as a sympathy plea, to procure a position. The lawyer then asked if Ishmael would call in a couple of days' time when he would be able to give him an answer. This looked hopeful and, after his work, back at home that evening, he told Hagar what he had done, feeling a little more optimistic that he could have the position with the lawyer. Two days later, he called at the office and was greeted by the lawyer. Looking straight at Ishmael, he paused and said he would give him a trial period to prove he could do the work and, if he found him satisfactory, he would make it permanent. Ishmael had always paid his rent in six-monthly sums.

The lawyer said to him, "You are one of my tenants,

aren't you?"

Ishmael replied, "Yes. We have an addition to the family. My wife has given me a boy, who is now five months old, and his name is Ibrahim."

The lawyer congratulated him and told him he could start his new position on the coming Monday. Ishmael was highly delighted at the thought of his new job. The lawyer had not said how much he would pay him, but it could not be less than he was getting at the garage, which reminded him that he must tell his employer then that he had decided to leave in the next few days.

*　*　*

In the meantime, things were not going well for Arun. He was busy sorting out lots of problems with 'settlers'. There were regular attacks by disenchanted Palestinians who had lost their land. It was a full-time occupation trying to stop the hit and run attacks and sniper fire by them. Some of the Jewish settlers had taken it upon themselves to counter attack their supposed enemies. One group had made an incursion into Palestine territory, and had attempted to blow up a mosque. In the process, they had killed some innocent bystanders, including children and women, causing more hatred and outrage. Arun was personally becoming disillusioned with the whole process. It had been nothing but violence since the day he had joined the army as a conscript. Generally, he liked his life, and it gave him many privileges and a good salary. He was now fifty-nine years old, and would be retiring when he reached the age of sixty. Ruth was nearing fifty-four years old. Both were still very sad after Deborah's— as they still called her— walk out. Every day, they hoped that she might get in touch with them. She was their only child. Even if she was considered an adult and they had no jurisdiction over her, she was the only remaining near relative they had, after the tragic loss of Arun's mother, then the death of his father, together with the sad loss of

Ruth's father, Usef, and her mother, Letitia.

Israel was still making rapid progress economically and, in many areas, they had little violence. On the whole, they had a good existence if they were away from the main trouble areas; these were confined to the cities like Jerusalem, the border with Lebanon, Syria, and if you lived adjacent to Gaza. These were the hot spots of dissatisfaction, and spawned recruits to the terror groups of Hamas and Hezbollah.

Ishmael was feeling in the good mood, having secured a position with the lawyer, and felt more secure in his mind. Hagar and Ibrahim were doing well. The camp was still shut off by the military, and was being covered every day by army patrols. Hagar was keen to get in touch with her mother. She wanted to tell her about her child, and knew she would be overjoyed to see her. She talked to Ishmael, and asked him what she should do. He said that, with the closure of the area into town, it would not be easy to visit Jerusalem, and they could not say where they were and would have to keep their location from their parents, for the time being, unless her parents reconciled with them, especially her father. What would both of them achieve, and suppose they were rejected? Ishmael knew he could not even approach his father. He was certain that his father, Ahmed, had meant what he'd said to him. They did have an idea that, if they could contact Ishmael's sisters— with whom they had trusted the secret of their elopement— by letter, they might pass a message to Ruth, who still did some of her shopping in the market in the eastern sector of Jerusalem. His sisters had seen Ruth when they were at their father's fruit and vegetable stand. Hagar knew what her mother's telephone number was. If Ishmael could get a letter and the telephone number to his sisters, they could still remain anonymous. They would not have to say where they were. On reflection, Ishmael said he did not think it would be a good idea to get his family involved, in case things went wrong, and he was sure his father would be very displeased if he knew of their intentions.

The area of the camp was still under surveillance by the military, and was shut off from the town. Everyone was stopped and searched if they wanted to leave. This made things difficult for the people who had no work outside the refugee camp, but those who had work or businesses in the town were closely vetted and allowed passage if they had the right papers and identity. This only applied to a small number of the camp occupants, who were mostly poor, having lost their land, houses and livelihood. Ishmael and Hagar were now in this category, having put themselves in this position. Once again, they had to think how they could communicate with Hagar's parents. A telephone call would be the answer, if they had a telephone, but they did not, and could not use a public call box in the town for fear of being questioned. Ishmael, being bright as ever, said perhaps the lawyer where he worked would let him use his telephone. He thought he could only ask him and see if he was willing for them to use it.

* * *

The next day at the office, Ishmael asked him if he could let his wife, whom the lawyer had never met, make a telephone call to Jerusalem where her mother and father lived.

For a moment, he paused, then asked, "Couldn't she write a letter?"

Ishmael then said that his wife wanted to speak to her mother personally, and tell her about their baby boy, Ibrahim. The lawyer smiled and said that he was willing to let them use his telephone on condition they paid the charge. Ishmael thanked him and arranged to bring Hagar to the office the next day. The following morning, after Ishmael had gone to work, Hagar asked her female neighbour if she would mind looking after her child for a short time while she went out, and said she would return as soon as she could. The woman was only too pleased to have the child. She had shown a great interest in him from

156

the start. Besides, it was good company for her to once again be caring for a boy, as she had two grown-up sons living in the town. Hagar said goodbye to her, kissed the boy, and left to go to the lawyer's office. On arriving, Ishmael introduced Hagar to the lawyer, whose eyes lighted up as he remarked what a beautiful woman she was. Hagar thanked him for the compliment.

Ishmael said, "Yes, she takes after her mother, who was part Palestinian and Lebanese."

The lawyer remarked that Lebanese women were the most beautiful, to his eyes. With the formalities over, Hagar went to the telephone on the lawyer's desk, picked it up, and dialled the number. Immediately the telephone rang, a voice answered, asking who was ringing. For a moment, Hagar was silent, and tears began to fall from her eyes.

Then, in a broken, emotional voice, she said, "Mother, it's your daughter, Deborah."

She asked her mother how she and her father were. In a faltering voice, Ruth replied they were well, but had gone through a nightmare not knowing what had happened to them all this time. Deborah said she was fine, and that Ishmael took good care of her. Also, she had some news to give her. Ruth was eager to know what the news could be.

"Are you coming back home?" she asked.

Deborah said that could not happen yet, because she had given birth to a baby boy called Ibrahim, who was now very near to his first birthday. She said she was well and happy, and hoped, as the boy grew and got stronger, that she would be able to bring him to see them, but, at the moment, she could not do that and did not want to give her location away. She reassured her mother that she still loved them both and, one day, they would meet again. Hagar said a tearful goodbye to her, then put down the telephone and thanked the lawyer for allowing her to call, saying farewell to the lawyer and Ishmael, who remained to continue his work. Ishmael felt relief that Hagar had dealt with what had been bothering her for a long time. She hurried back to the flat as quickly as she could. On returning, she went to her neighbour's flat, collected her son, and thanked the woman for her kindness. Before she could leave, the woman had noticed that Hagar had been crying, and still had the sign of tears in her eyes. Asking her what was upsetting her, Hagar replied she had become very emotional, as this was the first time she had talked with her mother since she had married, but, inside, she felt good having done so. The woman said the boy had been very good, and that she had enjoyed looking after him, and would do so again if the occasion arose.

As the days went by, things were beginning to get back to normal with the daily routine of looking after and caring for her son and Ishmael. The barriers had been removed between the town and the refugee camp, but there was still a military presence, with Israeli soldiers patrolling the area. Movement was not so restricted. It meant that Hagar and Ishmael could venture into the town of Hebron, and would be able to buy some new clothes for themselves and the baby. These goods were not easily available in the camp. The residents were very poor, and depended on charity handouts from Palestinian charities. Fortunately, Ishmael had quite a decent wage from the lawyer, so was able to have a better standard of living than some of his contemporaries.

*   *   *

As far as the rest of the world was concerned, it was still a cauldron of unrest. On their doorstep, Palestinians living on the West Bank were being more marginalised, and were subject to severe restrictions on their liberty. Israel justified this situation by blaming the terrorists from Hamas and Hezbollah, and other outside Islamic influences. Several countries were still embroiled in fighting for the cause they liked to call freedom, at the same time sucking Western nations into the mêlée to try to solve their grievances. These nations, in fact, exacerbated the situation and, every day, more innocent men, women and children died, and no one seemed to care. Israel was being reprimanded every day by the United Nations Assembly, but this had little effect on the way Israel was meting out what they considered to be punishment. The odds were heavily against the Palestinians who, in the Western world, had few supporters. However, amidst these acts of retribution, there were many Israelis who were very worried about how their military was operating. Voices were being heard from various groups of Israelis throughout the country; even from the country's parliament, the Knesset, there was unease. For the death of a small number of Jewish and army personnel, hundreds of innocent Palestinian men, women and children, and even babies, were being killed, but, still, neither party was willing to make any permanent settlement, so the killing went on.

Arun, who had been away in another region when Hagar had contacted her mother, received the news from Ruth about the telephone call. After hearing what she had said, Arun said he was pleased to hear that nothing had befallen her and Ishmael, and was pleased that they had a boy. His tone softened when he heard this. Although he was, at the time, not pleased with Deborah's actions, he was willing to welcome her home at any time, and be a family again. Life was going smoothly for Ishmael and Hagar. They were ready to celebrate Ibraham's first birthday, and put him through the Islamic ceremony that was traditional to Muslims. This would be arranged by the *imam* at the small local mosque and, after the ceremony, they would have friends and neighbours around for a celebration. Everything went according to Islamic laws. The boy was now one year old, and would grow up strong and healthy. Ishmael and Hagar hoped that there would be a better place for him, and he would be able to pursue coexistence with his neighbours. What was happening in other people's lives was not on Ishmael and Hagar's minds. They were concentrating on their own lives and that of

Ibrahim, their son. The days moved on. Both of them were quite happy with their lot. Sometimes, Hagar would ask Ishmael if he could think of a time when they would be able to visit her mother, Ruth, and let her see the boy. Ishmael suggested she should do that by herself, as he did not want to cause any friction between her parents and himself. Ibrahim was growing up fast. He was now approaching his second birthday, and would not find travelling too difficult. It was not a great distance from Hebron to Jerusalem. There were buses that operated between the two, and it was not expensive. A taxi would cost too much, and they could not afford to waste money on such a luxury. Hagar had made up her mind that she would travel with the boy, but she would not inform her mother that she would visit her. She said it would be a surprise for her, but she was uncertain how her father would react. As the restriction on the camp had been lifted, she told Ishmael not to worry about her travelling. She was, to everyone, just another Arab woman with a child.

* * *

Some days later, Hagar left Ishmael at his workplace and took a bus from inside the town. It would take her and Ibrahim at least two hours to reach Jerusalem. It was quite a change for her to travel outside the camp. She and Ishmael had virtually been isolated for the last two years, with the trouble in and around the area. After a tiring journey on the bus, she arrived a little exhausted, but excited. She was thinking how her parents would receive her and Ibrahim. Making her way from the bus stop, she walked towards the house where her parents lived. Cautiously, she approached the entrance and tapped upon the door. The door opened and, standing there, was her mother, Ruth. For a moment, both of them were speechless, then they hugged and kissed each other, both crying. Ruth ushered Deborah into the house, where they both sat and started talking about themselves. Ruth took hold of the boy, and said what a fine little boy he was. Deborah told her mother how they were living, and that Ishmael worked in a lawyer's office and they had quite a good living. Ruth was eager to know whereabouts they lived, but Deborah said that she and Ishmael had to keep it a secret in case Ishmael's father, Ahmed, found out. Even his sisters did not know exactly where they lived. Deborah asked her mother where her father was, and if he would be coming home that day or was away on duties somewhere. Ruth said he had taken a platoon of soldiers to an area to help the existing military. She did not know when he would return. She told Deborah that she was very upset and frightened in case anything happened to him. Deborah asked her mother how her father would react, knowing she had visited home. Ruth replied that, as he was nearing his retirement, his attitude had softened, and he had started to think like his father had about what was going on in Israel. He was getting disillusioned by the ongoing disturbances. He believed they were getting worse, and, whatever army actions were taken against the Palestinians and their outside supporters, it was not achieving a solution. He was glad he would not have to endure his stressful position for long, and was looking forward to being at his home permanently. Ruth said she thought that, in answer to Deborah's question as to what her father would say, she believed he would forgive her and would still support her if she needed it. Ruth asked Deborah what she intended to do now. Was she intending to return to where she and Ishmael lived, or, as it was getting late, she could stay with her for the night. Deborah did not anticipate staying away, especially as she had not told Ishmael that's what she might do. Her mother said it would be good if she did stay the night. Ruth said she often felt very lonely when Arun was away. She and the child would be good company for her. Deborah agreed to stay overnight and, at the same time, hoped that Ishmael would not get too worried about her. Ruth and Deborah had a lot to talk about. Deborah told her mother how happy she was with Ishmael. He was a good husband, kind and loving, and was not involved in any political or dissatisfied factions in the community.

They had a good night's rest and the boy was very well behaved. After a tearful goodbye to her mother, Deborah said she must return as quickly as she could. She knew that Ishmael would be worried about her. She kissed and held her mother for a while, then hurried away, at the same time saying she would get in touch with them again soon.

*　*　*

On returning home without incident, Hagar was pleased to see Ishmael, who had thought that she would possibly have stayed with her parents for the night. He was very pleased she and the boy were home again. Everything had been quite quiet and peaceful since the time the camp had been opened up again, but there were still soldiers and vehicles occasionally patrolling the streets. Ishmael arrived at work one day to find that his employer, the lawyer, was ill. His wife told Ishmael that he had told her the night before that he did not feel well. The lawyer was in his late forties, and was a little overweight. A doctor from the clinic had told him he thought he had suffered a heart attack, and should rest. This news worried Ishmael. Not only did he have sympathy for the man, but knew his job could be in jeopardy. Going home after his work, he relayed the news about the lawyer to Hagar, saying he could be out of work if anything disastrous befell him. At the moment, Ishmael was left to attend to the business. This was not too difficult to do, as he had learnt quite a lot from his employer during the two years he had worked there.

How long he would be doing this work depended on the whether or not the lawyer recovered. If he did not, or if he decided to give up the business, Ishmael would certainly be out of work. That was something he now had to worry about. Every day he went to the office, he was always apprehensive, wondering what to expect. As usual, he was greeted by the lawyer's wife, who looked very worried. Ishmael enquired how her husband was. She replied that he seemed to be a lot better. The doctor from the camp had paid a visit, and was satisfied that he could well recover, but he still had to take things easy. This was a relief to Ishmael. It meant that he could be in work, for the time being, at least.

At home that night, Hagar enquired how the lawyer was. Ishmael said that he had been visited by the clinic doctor, who said he thought he was much better, but he still had to rest. That meant that Ishmael would still have a job. Hagar was pleased to hear this. Ishmael picked up his son, Ibrahim, kissing him and making him laugh. Hagar looked on and said that he was spoiling the child, but in a nice way. Both Hagar and Ishmael were very happy. They had friendly neighbours, and everyone helped each other.

*　*　*

Hebron and the refugee camp had been quiet for the past few weeks. Life had been fairly normal, with only the occasional confrontation with the army patrols between youths and boys throwing stones and rocks at their vehicles. This seemed to be a kind of game for them. Sometimes, the boys were hit with plastic bullets, suffering an injury. Tear gas was occasionally used, if it was seen by the military to be getting out of hand, but this never had much effect on the youths, who continually taunted the Israeli soldiers. One morning, Ishmael went to work, as usual. On entering the lawyer's house, he saw quite a number of men and women, who all looked very distressed. Ishmael did not have to ask what the matter was. He knew something tragic had happened. It could only be that his employer had died. Now what would happen? He was yet to find out. He approached the lawyer's wife, expressed his sympathy at the loss of her husband, and asked if there was anything he could do.

She replied, "Not at present, but we will have to talk

after the funeral."

Ishmael went home, looking a little blank. Hagar asked him what had happened. He then told her about the lawyer, saying he was dead.

She asked, "Does that mean you won't have any work, Ishmael?"

Ishmael said he did not know until the lawyer had been buried, then his wife would let him know what the situation would be.

Ishmael paid his respects the next day, attending the funeral. Afterwards, the lawyer's wife said she would let him know her plans in a few days. As she had no family, she wanted time to think about her future. In the meantime, she asked if Ishmael would complete any outstanding letters and anything else that was pending in the business. He agreed to do this, and would wait for her decision.

* * *

The fragile peace was to be broken again. Fierce fighting had broken out in South Lebanon. The Israeli army had crossed into the area to quell acts of terrorism. At the same time, the Palestinian refugee camps were harbouring important guerrilla leaders from Hezbollah and allied groups. The Israelis targeted houses and places where these people were hiding, and carried out strikes against them. They had some success with this, but it was to the detriment of the civilian population, which suffered many deaths. Israel eventually drew back their forces after requests from the United Nations. Palestine had other factions, such as Fatah, which were moderate in their intentions, but they were being opposed by groups like Hamas, who were not in any compromising mood and insisted that only armed aggression towards the Israelis was the solution to recover their land. In this climate of hate and mistrust by both Jews and Palestinians, nothing was being achieved but more misery and grief. How long would this go on? No one had an answer.

Meanwhile, Ruth, who had been uplifted by the visit of her daughter, Deborah, was feeling less depressed, and was wishing the days and months away when Arun would no longer have to be away in the military. In another year, he would be able to retire. Ruth had found it very difficult to live with the constant fear of what could happen to him. Although the fighting was still going on in various areas of the country, it had been fairly peaceful between Hamas and supporters of Hezbollah, who were being backed by Syria, making the country once again very unstable. There were still troublesome areas in Israel and Palestine, in places like Gaza and the West Bank. Although Gaza was isolated from Palestine, it was in turmoil, with different factions all wanting to control the place and making incursions into Israel, causing problems for them. Most of the fighting in the West Bank was being made worse by the continuous building of Jewish settlements and the displacement of the Palestinians from their land. Universally, this was looked upon as a crime. Palestinians were being made refugees, while Israel was allowing more and more Jewish groups to enter the country to occupy these new dwellings. Resentment by the Palestinians caused them to harass and make trouble for the settlers. The Israeli parliament ignored any criticism, and carried on building, but the government, too, had its critics. Some members thought they were going, or had gone, too far with this policy, but they were a minority and were always overruled by the hard-line members.

*   *   *

It would soon be Christmas. The city of Jerusalem was beginning to fill with different religious groups, all wanting to worship at their own holy places. The Israelis, at this time of year, were extremely cautious, and had put heavy security in place. The last thing they wanted was an outbreak of terrorism. With so many people about, it would be disastrous for them.

Arun, whose HQ was near the city, was involved in this security, and told Ruth that he hoped everything would be peaceful during the period.

Ishmael, in the meantime, was waiting for a decision by the lawyer's wife about what she was going to do regarding the business. A few days went past. Ishmael went to the office. When he arrived, the lawyer's wife said she did not want to carry on with her husband's work; she could not do it, and she did not want to be involved anymore. She told Ishmael she was getting too old now to bother with it. She was sorry that Ishmael would have to find some other work. She would settle up with him, and pay him the money he was owed. Ishmael asked about the flats owned by her husband.

"As I am in one, does that mean I will have to leave?"

She replied, "No."

She said that now that her husband had passed away, she would be the owner of the block of flats he was in. The rent would give her an income for her living. Ishmael told her he was pleased that he would still have a home. He thanked the woman, saying he had enjoyed working with her husband.

"I will soon find another position," said Ishmael.

He then left to return home to Hagar and Ibrahim. Returning home, he was welcomed by Hagar and his son, as usual, but, this time, the smile had left his face, and he looked quite thoughtful. Hagar asked if there was something wrong.

Ishmael replied, "Not exactly, but I can tell you that I do not have a job anymore. The lawyer's wife is giving up her husband's business, so it means the end for me. Now I have to find some work soon, or we will be in trouble."

Hagar told him he would soon be able to do that, as he was very good at most tasks. She suggested that he may be able to get his work back at the garage, or he could go into town and try to find a position. As he had worked for a lawyer, perhaps he may be lucky finding one who would employ him. Losing his job did not help matters. He and Hagar were constantly thinking about their families, whom they had not seen or, in Ishmael's case, had not had contact with, for quite a long time. He often wondered how they were managing. He knew his father would not suffer too much, being a businessman. Sometimes, Ishmael thought that, if things had been different, he would have a business, like his father, and would be wealthy, but he had a loving wife and a fine, strong son. What more could he want?

*　*　*

The Christmas period was now over, and a New Year arrived. Arun was pleased that Jerusalem had not suffered any terrorist attacks, but that was not the case in other parts of the country. Most of the troubles were confined to the Gaza Strip, where in-fighting by political groups was occurring. They were also making life difficult for the Israeli army and the Jewish settlers outside the surrounding area, firing rockets— most of which were homemade, but still quite devastating— causing damage and deaths. Of course, these acts were quickly followed by the army making forays into the town and inflicting air strikes, with the same consequences; killing, they said, targeted terrorist leaders, but causing numbers of women, children and ordinary civilian casualties. Many nations were now voicing opinions, saying the Israelis were too heavy handed at dealing with these outbreaks, and pleas were made, even by some of their friends, both American and European, but most of these requests were being ignored.

Arun and Ruth were looking forward to the New Year, 1998, the year he would retire. He would be sixty years old, and Ruth would be fifty-four. Ruth would be glad that her husband would not have to be away for long periods anymore. Indeed, their lives would be their own, not the army's, in future and so they could do as they pleased. Also, they would be financially sound with Arun's pension.

Ishmael had taken Hagar's advice, and had gone to see the owner of the garage where he had once worked, but, to his dismay, it no longer existed as a garage. It had now become a shop selling local fruit, vegetables, and other groceries. This was a disappointment to Ishmael. Now he would have to go into the town of Hebron and enquire about work, as there would be no work available in the camp. Setting off, he went first to the business area, which he could see was predominantly Jewish. He looked around, and found what he took to be lawyer's premises, by the notices on them. As he had always worn Western-type clothing, he would not look unusual to anyone, as most of the people moving around were similarly dressed, except the Orthodox Jews, who were wearing their own particular clothes. Entering one of the offices, he asked one of the people there if he could speak to the owner. At that moment, a man appeared, asking Ishmael what he wanted.

Ishmael asked, "Are you the owner?"

The man replied, "Yes, I am."

Ishmael said he was looking for a position with a lawyer. His previous job was in a lawyer's office, but, unfortunately, his employer had died. The man asked him if he was Palestinian.

Ishmael replied, "Yes."

The man then asked, "Was your last employer Palestinian, too?"

Ishmael again said, "Yes."

The man replied, "Why would you want to work for a Jew?"

Ishmael said he was not prejudiced against anyone. His family had lived for generations alongside Jews. His father was a businessman, a market trader, and many of his customers were from the Jewish community. Besides, he himself was married to a Jewish girl, whose father was an Israeli, and whose mother was half Palestinian and Christian Lebanese.

"Are you qualified as a lawyer?" the man asked.

"No," said Ishmael, "but I learnt a lot from my last employer, although most of my work consisted of writing letters to clients and other clerical work."

"Have you tried to obtain a position anywhere else?" the man asked.

"No," replied Ishmael. "You are the first person I have seen."

The man then said, "We already have a man working here for us, who is a Jordanian. I suggest you come back tomorrow again. In the meantime, I will speak to my partner in the business."

Ishmael went back home feeling optimistic that, again, he could be lucky and procure a job. Hagar and Ibrahim were keen to know how he had fared in the town. Ishmael told her everything that had happened, and hoped everything would go well for them. Hagar said there had been a disturbance in the camp while he was away. The neighbour had told her that a military vehicle on the road out of the camp had been wrecked by a bomb, killing three Israeli soldiers. They had arrested two Arabs or Palestinians whom they thought had caused it, as they had been seen running away from the scene towards the camp, but had been caught by one of the army patrols who were in the camp. This was disturbing news to Ishmael. He hoped they would not shut off access to the camp; otherwise, it would certainly spoil his chance of work in the town. Things quietened down, and Ishmael was relieved that the Israelis had not closed access to the camp, so he would be able to keep his appointment with the lawyer.

On the morning of the next day, he left Hagar and Ibrahim, telling her that, if he was not back early, it was possible that he had been given the position at the law firm office. The lawyer asked Ishmael exactly the same questions as his previous employer had asked. He assured him that he had never been involved in any trouble with the authorities, and had no criminal record of any description. The man seemed to accept his word, and said he would employ him as a clerk, but he would not be able to make any legal decisions. Ishmael was quite happy to do this. He was pleased that he now had work, and would be earning a living again. When he got home that evening, the smile on his face told Hagar what she wanted to know.

* * *

Other places in the country were still having the usual, never-ending problems with the settlers and the extension of settlements on the West Bank of Palestine. Palestinian groups from Ramallah were carrying out attacks on them, with the Israelis counter attacking them, which, inevitably, caused more bloodshed and sorrow to innocent people. The town of Hebron was having a respite from trouble, and Ishmael had settled down in his new job. His Jewish employer found him very capable and intelligent, which made Ishmael feel good. Also, he was receiving more money than he had before. On his way back from the town, he would stop at a shop or store and buy something for Hagar and Ibrahim, who was growing up quite quickly, and was now walking and talking. With all the problems around them, Hagar and Ishmael were happy and, from such a poor start, considered themselves very fortunate. The only thing they did worry about was their parents and what was happening to them. Hagar had promised her mother that she would keep in contact with her. She asked Ishmael, as he worked in an office, if he could, perhaps, write a letter for her to send to her mother. Ishmael said he could do that, if she could tell him what she wanted put in the letter. Of course, her mother may be able to find out where they lived, but it would only give the postal town. She would not know where they actually were. Hagar wrote down what she wanted Ishmael to write, and gave it to him to take the next day.

Hagar did not hear from her mother, as she did not have an address, but she was sure that her mother would know she and the boy were well. There had been another disturbance in the town, in Jerusalem. In Hebron, a small bomb had been detonated in a café. It had not killed anyone, but had injured a small number of diners. Ishmael was worried that the refugee camp could again be closed off. What would he do then? Fortunately, nothing happened. That was a great relief for him. It was more serious in Jerusalem. A Jewish man had gone into a mosque and opened fire, killing people at prayer. He was arrested by the Israelis and taken away. This episode had the effect of infuriating the Palestinians, who came out in numbers into the street in protest. A few shots were fired, but there were no casualties. The Israeli forces confined the situation and calmed everything down. This was happening on Arun's doorstep and it worried him a great deal. Soon, in less than seven months, he would retire, and would not be part of the violence anymore. Like a lot of his Israeli contacts, he was getting fed up with the day-to-day violence throughout the land, with no solution in sight. Numbers of Jews had decided to leave Israel, going back to the countries they had originally left, even those countries that were once their persecutors and enemies. They left not for economic reasons, but because they could see no end to the violence, and an uncertain future in Israel.

Although the Palestine and Israel situation was calm, except for spasmodic outburst of terrorism, Lebanon was not so lucky, and was still a thorn in the Israelis' side. Also, there still existed political turmoil, with different parties claiming control, some supported by outside influences. Some hope had emerged in other places. The Irish, who had a parallel grievance with the Palestinians, eventually reached an agreement to share power in the Ulster Union, but for how long? Like the situation in Israel, it was in the lap of the gods.

* * *

It had been several weeks since the last incident, and Ishmael had left every day to go into the town to work in the lawyer's office. He was enjoying his work. His

Jewish employers were very good to him, giving him time off on Jewish holy days. This enabled him to go about with Hagar and Ibrahim and enjoy a little leisure. This way of life, for them, was to come to an abrupt end. A riot broke out in the refugee camp. It had been taken over by an armed group believed to be Arab gunmen who were allied to Hezbollah or Hamas. These insurgents were putting fear into the residents. The Israeli army, which was patrolling the camp, was coming under fire from snipers who were hiding or taking cover in residents' houses. This was a classic use of 'human shields' and it made things very difficult for the Israeli Army to retaliate with women and children vulnerable to death or injury.

Returning home, Ishmael was disturbed to find that the army was stopping people who were entering the camp. Having produced his pass, Ishmael was allowed to go home. He was eager to see his wife and son, fearing that something may have happened to them. He was very relieved to find nothing was amiss. If the trouble got worse, he would not be able to get to work. After all, the good fortune he had enjoyed for the last eighteen months could be abruptly coming to an end. To add to his worries, that night, a gun battle between the gunmen and the army patrol broke out, causing all the people on the street to take cover, and sheltering in their houses to avoid being involved. Ishmael and Hagar talked to each other. If the worst came, what would he do for work? The camp had just one or two small shops and a few cafés. They could not offer him any viable employment. During the night, occasional gunfire could be heard, which was not a good sign. The next morning, Ishmael ventured out into the street. He could see two or three armed vehicles, and soldiers standing around them. He told Hagar that he would try to go to work.

She said, "I hope things don't get worse, else you will have no work."

Ishmael kissed his wife and child, and set off down the strect. He was immediately stopped by an Israeli policeman, who asked him for his pass, asking where he was going and why. Ishmael said he was going to work at a lawyer's office in the town, and gave the policeman the name of the place where he worked as a clerk. He said his employers were Jewish, who were very good people to work for. The policeman gave him back his pass, and told him he could proceed. Again, Ishmael was glad he could go.

The hold up with the policeman made him a little late arriving. He apologised to his employer, explaining what had been going on at the camp. His apology and reasons were accepted, and he settled down to his work. He had no trouble in returning home, where he was welcomed by his wife and the boy. Hagar remarked that there had been more gunshots, but they had been at the other end of the camp. Ishmael went to work the next day without any problem, but it was a different story when he returned. There were many more soldiers and vehicles around. He was again stopped as he approached the camp, then asked for his pass. He was asked if he lived in the camp.

"Yes," he replied. "I have lived there for more than two years, but I work in the town."

He was let through. Apparently, a gun battle had taken place while he was at work. A number of the gunmen who had ventured into the open had been killed, and two Israeli soldiers had been badly wounded. Ishmael learnt that they had put a curfew in place, and no one was being allowed into the camp, except with food, cooking gas, and water. Also, no one could leave. The army had sent more troops to rout out the gunmen, who they estimated were quite a number. Ishmael was devastated. This could put an end to his job. How would he be able to keep his wife and boy, without work? The next day, there were more battles between the gunmen and the army, who found it very difficult to find the culprits who were hiding in ordinary people's homes, often with the consent of the families who were there, and not well disposed to the Israelis who were instrumental in depriving them of their land and livelihood. Ishmael was not going to give up. He decided to leave the camp, but was refused, even after explaining that he was employed by a Jewish firm. Disappointed, he returned home, feeling depressed. However, Hagar was optimistic that the curfew would be lifted in a couple of days.

*　*　*

A week had come and gone, and everyone in the refugee camp was getting impatient with the army still upholding the curfew. Occasional gunfire was still going on, and many more people were coming out on the streets, protesting to the soldiers. Children and youths were antagonising them, throwing rocks and stones at them, whilst the soldiers invariably retaliated with tear gas, making the youths more determined to taunt them. Ishmael knew he would not have his job if the curfew went on for much longer. A few days passed and, as the gunmen seemed to have made their escape or departure, the Israelis lifted the curfew. Ishmael was desperate to leave the camp and get into town to see if he still had his job. Saying goodbye to Hagar and Ibrahim, he set off to the lawyer's office. On arriving, he was greeted by his employer, who said he had heard about the trouble in the camp. To Ishmael's relief, he said he could carry on working. Thanking the lawyer for letting him back, he got down to his task as a clerk.

Life was getting back to normal for Hagar and Ishmael. The days went quite quickly, and the boy, Ibrahim, was doing well and growing. Hagar still worried what her parents were doing; whether they were well or if anything had befallen them. She knew, from reports, that there were still troublesome areas. The cause of this was mainly due to the continuous expropriation of Palestinian land and property for the extension of the settler's dwellings, which seemed to continue unabated, adding fuel to the fire of hate and despair by the Palestinians, who did not have the allies to support them, except half-hearted attempts by a few nations who were not affected politically or economically by their plight. The few supporters they had did not have a strong enough voice to alter or change minds, which was now a normal happening. Riots were breaking out again in Gaza, Ramallah and Lebanon. After a peaceful period, it was too good to be true. All of the troubles were not entirely aimed at the Israelis. Factions of Palestinian groups were at odds with each other, trying to put each other's points and actions against each party, resorting to violence with each other. It pleased the Israelis to see them disagreeing with one another. It meant that they were disorganised, and would have no power if they were politically and practically fragmented. It gave the Israelis breathing space to assess their position, but it did considerable harm for the Palestinians to achieve any goal or political settlement. With aspirations, promise and hope, Arun's father, Daniel, if he was still alive, would be hoping that Palestine and Israel would have reached an amicable agreement on partition by now, which could make the country a 'Land of Milk and Honey', but only his son and family would know it was still flowing with blood and tears, with more to come.

* * *

Leaving his workplace one evening, Ishmael heard a terrific explosion. He could tell it was not in the camp, but somewhere in the centre of town. Without wasting time to find out, he hurried back to Hagar, knowing if the explosion had been committed or thought to be have committed by Palestinians or Arabs, the Israelis would be arresting whoever they considered suspects. He got back to his house and, sure enough, a number of tanks and vehicles appeared from everywhere. They learnt over the radio that two suicide bombers had blown themselves up, one in a bus full of Israelis, and another inside a car outside a shopping centre, in total, killing thirty people and wounding many more. This, to the Israelis, was an outrage, and they were going to take revenge on the perpetrators who had

175

organised it. The first place to look was the camp. With the recent forays with the gunmen, it would be the obvious place, to them. Again, the camp was closed off, meaning that Ishmael would again be unable to leave. A strict night and evening curfew was once again put in place, this time more rigid than before. The Israelis believed that the camp was the hiding place for the bombers, as it was close to the town, and it was unlikely they would have travelled any distance, being fitted with explosives.

Ishmael was getting very miserable with what was going on. It seemed he would not have his job back. It was beginning to look like the military was going to be around for some time. With only the usual survival goods allowed into the camp, no one was allowed to leave. It was fortunate that Ishmael had saved a little money. At least he could pay his landlady the rent for their flat, and buy food for themselves and the boy. Days went past with no let up on the curfew. There were still some incidents with sniper fire from various points in the camp, which caused the soldiers more aggravation, especially as they did not come from the same place all the time.

More than three weeks had gone past, but the curfew remained. Ishmael was resigned to the fact that he had no work to go to. It was certain, with the recent outrage in the town centre, that the lawyer would not make him welcome again, as he was a Palestinian. Ishmael was at a loose end and, to occupy his time, had started to frequent a café just near his flat, and sat with one or two young people who also had nothing to do. They just sat in the café, drinking coffee and listening to the old and middle-aged men who seemed to spend most of their time there. Ishmael and his friends would listen to them recounting the days when they had lived on their own land, telling stories of how they lived, saying that they grew plenty of vegetables, and had a small vineyard on three or four hectares of land. They also had goats and sheep, and were self-sufficient, having their own milk and meat to sustain them. They were bemoaning the fact that their livelihood had been taken from them, but declared, by the will of Allah, they would one day recover their birthright. Ishmael listened intently to them, and was impressed with their optimism. What was really on Ishmael's mind, however, was how he was going to earn a living. One of the men in the café who had befriended him said he might be able to find him a job. He said he worked for a tanner who collected goat and sheep skins from the *Halaal* butcher. He prepared them and sold them to a Jewish company in the town, who then manufactured certain items like bags and footwear. If Ishmael was prepared to get his hands dirty, it did not pay much money, but it was a living. The man told Ishmael that he would enquire if he could be employed, and would let him know.

Ishmael went home and told Hagar about what his friend had said. He had to do something, even if it was temporary. Hagar agreed that even a small amount of money would be acceptable, as they were nearing the end of the meagre savings they had. Meeting in the café the next day, his friend told Ishmael that he could have work at the tannery, and warned him it was quite a dirty and smelly job, and many had left because of that. Ishmael said he was prepared to do the work. He went the next day to the tannery on the outskirts of the camp, where the employer said he could start work right away. After some help and instructions, Ishmael soon picked up the process of dealing with the smelly skins. When he arrived back home at night, he was glad to wash and rid himself of the smell from the tannery. Hagar had a laugh at Ishmael. She thought it was funny. Ishmael also joined in her humour, and they agreed it was better to smell a little and have some money than to have nothing.

It was obvious that the camp was still going to be under a curfew. Almost every day, you could hear gunfire. It was uncertain who was doing the firing. Some occupants of the camp were joining the gunmen who were still there, mainly because of the situation of virtually being prisoners, with no freedom of movement.

*   *   *

Ishmael stuck at his job, knowing that, at least, he had a little money coming in. He only worked for three days a week at the tannery, and really would have liked to have another job to bring in a little more money. In the café one day, he again got into conversation with a man who repaired old motor vehicles. Ishmael mentioned to him that he had worked at a garage on the outskirts of the town, but had lost his job because the garage was now a shop selling vegetables and other things. The man said he worked by himself and had a lot of repairs to be done. If Ishmael could help him out, he would pay him an amount, but it was not a lot, as he did not make a great deal of money. Ishmael accepted his offer, and would work for two days in the week.

At home, Ishmael told Hagar about his talk with the man at the café, saying it would boost his wages from the tannery, and would keep their heads above water until things were back to normal. Hagar, as usual, looked after their son, Ibrahim, and took him around the camp. She now knew many of the women who lived nearby, and would stop with the boy and talk to them. As she was fluent in Arabic, this was not difficult for her. Doing a little shopping at one of the small shops, she thought she would buy some flowers. It was a long time since she had purchased any; besides, it would cheer up the look of the house, and Ishmael. At home, she arranged the flowers in a vase, and put them on the balcony of the flat, so that they could be seen better than in a dark room. Ishmael arrived home from the tannery, smelly, as usual, and eager to change and clean himself. He asked Hagar if anything of any importance had happened. She told him nothing had, but that she had been into the camp, and, although there were still quite a number of soldiers about, it had been a quiet day. Ishmael noticed the flowers on the balcony, and asked Hagar, "Why did you have to buy those? You know we cannot afford luxuries like flowers."

She said, "I thought it would cheer us up in the midst of things that are happening."

Ishmael said, "Nothing much will cheer me up in our present state of affairs. I just want to get back to a decent job and live our normal lives."

Hagar looked a little sad, and got on with preparing the nightly meal for Ishmael and Ibrahim.

* * *

The next day, it was back to work for Ishmael at the tannery, with its smells and dirt. Hagar left the flat and took the boy with her. It was good for him to have the exercise. This time, she went further into the camp. Suddenly, there was a terrific bang. A rocket landed, seemingly out of nowhere into a house, all but demolishing it. It was probably aimed at a tank with the Israeli crew standing around it. Everybody instantly disappeared off the street. Hagar and the boy took shelter in one of the houses. Then, mayhem broke loose. There was shooting and sniper fire from all around. The army was firing in the direction of the gunfire. Every now and then, the gunmen would come into the street with their faces covered, and would confront the soldiers. A tank opened fire further up the road at a building where a lot of gunfire was coming from, causing some female occupants to come out, shouting and screaming at the soldiers. One woman was carrying a small child in her arms, who had suffered wounds from the collapsing building, which was still hiding some gunmen who were not surrendering. The sound of gunfire seemed to be everywhere; coming from all directions. This was a major battle between the army and the gunmen. The army believed that quite a number of insurgents had entered the camp, somehow, and were being joined by some camp occupants, mostly young Palestinians. The battle was getting louder. Tanks were abolishing any building that housed the gunmen. Now many civilians were also being

179

drawn into the fray, risking their lives.

Unfortunately, some did suffer wounds. No one would know if any had been killed until it ended. Hagar was still holed up in a house, and was frightened to venture out. More tanks came into the camp; it was beginning to resemble a battlefield. The gunfire from the infiltrators and army never seemed to stop. Hagar, at this stage, did not know what was happening or where Ishmael was. She hoped there would be a lull in the fighting, then she would make her way back to the flat. It must have been an hour later that the firing near her shelter stopped. Hagar ventured out with the boy, into the street. She had not got far when, from some houses on one side of the street, sniper fire began. A soldier was hit, falling to the ground a distance away. His comrades rushed to pick him up, and sheltered behind one of the tanks. More gunfire was being targeted at the tanks and the vehicles full of soldiers. Hagar took a chance, and ran with the boy. As she ran, the firing was still going on. The first tank that she neared opened fire towards the opposite side of the street. Hagar held onto the boy and made a dash. Bending as low as she could, suddenly, she dropped to the ground. She had been hit by a bullet from the direction of the tank. Someone got out of the tank. The firing ceased, and some women came running out into the street and gathered around Hagar. The officer from the tank approached the women to see what had happened. He looked at Hagar, who was dead. His face went white. He said nothing as the women threatened him, calling him a murderer.

* * *

Arun was completely stunned. Unknowingly, he had killed his own daughter. He returned to the tank, and ordered the patrol away from the area. By some unknown factor, the gunfire stopped throughout the camp. Ishmael had been told that a young woman with a small boy had been killed. He panicked and, although some distance away, raced down the street to where the women were standing around Hagar's body. Some were praying; some were weeping. Ishmael got to the place where his wife was. The first thing he saw was a woman holding the child's hand. He took hold of the boy and looked down. To his horror, he could see it was his wife, Hagar. He became overcome with grief, and hugged and kissed her, with tears streaming down his face. The women tried to console him, saying that he must think about his son, and they would take his wife into one of their houses until the next day. Ishmael was reluctant to let his wife go, but the women gently eased him from her and, still with tears coming down his face, he took the boy by the hand and slowly made his way back to the flat. He was about to have another shock. As he approached it, he could see a gaping hole in his flat, above the balcony. His neighbour's flat was also damaged. He was now numbed by the events that had been inflicted upon him. His neighbours greeted him as he entered the flat, and asked where his wife was. Ishmael could hardly speak; he was so overcome by losing his beautiful wife. It was a great effort to even mention that his wife was dead. The neighbours were very sympathetic to him, and expressed their condolences, saying they would miss his wife a lot. They were such good friends. Ishmael composed himself after the neighbours said that they would help him if he needed anything. He thanked them for their offer, then asked them what had happened to their flats. The neighbour said two gunmen had been on the roof of the flats. The army had not been able to dislodge them. Somehow, they had taken refuge in Ishmael's flat and commenced firing again. That was when the army had fired at them with the tank gun, doing the damage, but the gunmen had managed to escape.

Ishmael and the boy entered the flat. He looked around at the chaos that the tank had caused, and felt totally drained. He found some food for his son, and made a drink for himself. He went with Ibrahim to get a chair that was undamaged, and sat with the boy. Whilst sitting there, he noticed the vase of flowers on the floor of the balcony. Suddenly, tears came to his eyes again. He was becoming very emotional. He remembered telling Hagar that she should not have bought the flowers. He now regretted this. He got up, went to the balcony and picked up the vase, which, miraculously, had not broken. He picked up the flowers, one by one, and, with their heads drooping, placed them in the vase.

The boy got up, took his father's hand, and asked, "Why are the flowers crying, Daddy? Are they crying for Mummy?"

Ishmael picked his son up and hugged him, with tears streaming from his eyes. He put the boy down again, then said to him, "We will have to get the house tidy and get some sleep."

Before doing anything else, Ishmael had to think about what he had to do about his wife's burial. Although she had adopted Islam, in a way, she had been brought up in the Jewish faith. Not being able to leave the camp, he approached an officer with some soldiers, who were still patrolling the camp. Ishmael asked him if he could see or be in touch with a rabbi. The officer asked him why.

He then said, "The army has killed my wife. Although I am a Palestinian, she was born a Jew, and brought up in that faith. She must be buried soon, and I wish her to have a Jewish burial."

The officer motioned a vehicle to him, saying to Ishmael, "Take me where your wife is now."

Ishmael got in the vehicle with the boy, and they set off to the house where the women had taken Hagar. Knocking at the door, a woman answered, asking what they wanted. Then she recognised Ishmael. He said he had come to take his wife. He then went inside, and saw that Hagar was completely wrapped up, ready for burial. The officer said he would take the body to a synagogue and see the rabbi, who would arrange the burial. He regretted that Ishmael would not be able to go with them, as nobody was allowed to leave the camp, which was still under curfew.

Ishmael bent and put his arms around his wife, and again became quite emotional. The officer assured Ishmael she would be treated with respect, and would have a Jewish burial the next day. Ishmael picked up Hagar's body, and gently and laid it in the vehicle. The officer then drove out of the camp. There was nothing more that Ishmael could do, so he picked up his son. He thanked the women in the house for their sympathy and kindness, and made his way back to his flat, with intense sorrow weighing on his shoulders.

The next day, after a sleepless night, Ishmael was still distraught and upset by the loss of his wife, Hagar, whom he loved very much. He could not decide what to do. Should he go back to work at the tannery, or should he get in touch with his father again? What would his father's attitude be to him? He had had no contact for more than three years. Would he welcome him and his son back? His father was very anti-Jewish, even though he made a living from their patronage at his business in the market. Ishmael decided to give himself some time to think of what his best course of action was. He had to concentrate on his son at the moment. Talking to his neighbour, who had kindly offered to help him with getting the flat to a liveable standard, he told him he would like to go back to work now that it seemed the crisis had diminished, but what about his son? He would have to give up work and look after him. At the same time, he had to have money to keep them both. The neighbour said that, if he wanted to go back to work, he was sure his wife would look after the boy for him while he was away. She liked to have children around. It gave her a lot of pleasure, and she had known the boy since he had been born.

Ishmael took on a more positive determination to get on with his life. He had lost his wife, but still had part of her with his son.

* * *

Arun, being in the position he held as a senior officer, had left the camp and had returned to his HQ in Jerusalem. Arriving back home, he entered the house, looking very depressed. Ruth welcomed him with open arms. She was very pleased to see him back safely. As she held him, he seemed to give no response to her emotions. Ruth stood back and asked him what was wrong.

"Why are you so pale, and shaking?"

Arun said he had some dreadful news to give her.

She asked, "Has something gone wrong in your HQ or the army?"

It took Arun several seconds to reply. He said, "Not with the army, although they played a part in it. It gives me a lot of pain and sorrow to tell you that our daughter, Deborah, is dead."

Ruth was shocked, turning pale and agitated, and asked, "Are you sure? How do you know this?"

Arun composed himself. He took Ruth's hand. Ruth, who now looked as if she had seen a ghost, sat. Arun told her that the camp at Hebron had got out of hand with rioting and gunmen rampaging through it, causing casualties to the army personnel. In the emergency, he went with a platoon and his tanks to ascertain the trouble. During the exchange of gunfire with some snipers, a woman with a child was caught in the crossfire. She fell in front of his tank, hit by a bullet. He got out and was totally shocked and dumbstruck looking at the woman in Arab dress. He immediately recognised Deborah. He could not do or say anything, as a number of women had come on the scene and shouted insults and threats against him and his soldiers. His only option was to leave, not revealing he was her father, so he had left quickly, returning to Jerusalem. He was not certain whether the bullet came from his men in his tank or one of the snipers. He felt he must take the blame for her death. Arun took Ruth by the hand, and looked at her. She had tears running down her face. He comforted her, and kept asking, "Why did this have to happen?" After a pause of quietness, Arun suddenly raised his voice, and asked, "How much more of this Hell must we suffer? Will it never end?"

They now had to find out what had happened to their beautiful daughter, and what would happen to her son, their grandchild.

They did not have long to wait. A few days later, a letter arrived for them from Ishmael, saying how devastated he was with the loss of his wife, Hagar. He would always miss her, because he loved her so much. He said in his letter that, although she had adopted some Islamic practices, out of respect for them, Arun, and her mother, Ruth, she had been given a Jewish burial, with a rabbi in attendance. He was sure that's what she would have wanted. Arun and Ruth felt comforted by the letter. They at least knew that their daughter had had a proper Jewish burial, with respect. Ishmael, by the kindness of his neighbour looking after his son, resumed his work at the tannery and helping his friend repair cars. He did not know how long he could do that, but he needed the money. There was nothing else he could do in the camp, so he may try to leave one day to give his son a better life.

The camp had been without any outbreaks of violence and gunfire, so the army had lifted the curfew, which meant that Ishmael and his son, Ibrahim, could go into the town, and his son could see more of the world than the refugee camp. Ishmael made up his mind to get in touch with his sisters in Jerusalem, telling them what had happened to him, and the tragedy that had befallen him, explaining what had taken place, and telling them that he had a small son and was living in a refugee camp, finding it difficult to find any work or earn enough money. He asked them to approach his father, Ahmed, and see if he was prepared to forgive him for the past, and to tell him his son's name was Ibrahim, which might please him. They could telephone him at a certain time. His landlady, the lawyer's wife, had a telephone, and he was sure she would let him use it.

* * *

Some days had passed. The situation was beginning to worry Ishmael. He was now desperate for any news. He had not had the telephone call that he had arranged with his sisters, and wanted to know why. He waited a few more days for them to get in touch with him, but he heard nothing. Ishmael decided he would take a chance and go to Jerusalem to call on his sisters. He asked the friend he helped repair cars if he would let him borrow one for him to visit his relatives in Jerusalem. Although he had not driven a car on the road for some time, he was sure that he was still able. His friend agreed, but said he had to buy the fuel for it, and not to crash it. Ishmael told him he would go the next day, and get back as soon as he could.

The next morning, Ishmael set off for Jerusalem with his son, feeling anxious about what sort of reception he may receive. On his way, he had some narrow escapes. He did not realise that the traffic had increased so much. He reminded himself he had to be careful, or he may endanger his son. It was seventy kilometres from Hebron to Jerusalem, and it would take him about two hours to reach his sisters' house.

Eventually, he arrived without any mishap. Driving down the narrow street where they lived, he found the house, stopped outside, took the boy from the car, and knocked at his sisters' door. They opened the door to him, and were surprised to see Ishmael standing there with his son. Both his sisters welcomed him with open arms, hugging and weeping at the same time. They invited him in and, looking at Ibrahim, exclaimed what a nice looking boy he was. After the greetings and welcome was over, Ishmael got down to the business of enquiring why they had not responded to his letter, and asked what his father has said. His sisters replied that their father was not at home at present. He had gone to visit his brother in Tel Aviv, and would not be back for a few days yet. Ishmael was a little disappointed. He said he had to return to Hebron, because

186

he had borrowed the car from a friend, and had promised he would return it to him the same day. After his sisters had fed him and the boy, Ishmael gave them the address and telephone number of the lawyer's office where he had worked, saying that the deceased lawyer's wife would let him know of their correspondence or telephone calls. He saw her quite often, as she owned the flat he lived in. He paid her rent once a month. Ishmael said goodbye to his sisters, telling them to speak to his father when he returned.

*   *   *

Arun and Ruth were still very upset with what had happened. Now it would only be two months before Arun retired, and he couldn't wait for it to come. Then, they may be able to reorganise their lives. Still, in certain areas like the West Bank and Gaza, the fighting and protests were still prevalent, with the usual results of more deaths, the majority being Palestinians. Also, settlers were sometimes having a lot of problems with snipers and occasional rocket attacks. The Palestinians were now at a disadvantage. Israel was a well-armed and efficient force, with a well-equipped army and air power, which was having a deterrent effect on the gunmen and their leaders. This was creating a semblance of stability and Israel, as a nation, was prospering into a modern and economic state, whilst the Palestinians were still having problems with their political leaders and breakaway groups. Ishmael called in to the lawyer's old office to see if there had been any letter for him. To his surprise, the woman said she did, indeed, have a letter for him. Ishmael became excited, and quickly opened the envelope. Reading it, a smile came upon his face. His father had told his sisters that he would forgive him for running away, because of the grief he had suffered with the loss of his wife, he was willing for him to come back into the family, and was eager to see his grandson. This was good news for Ishmael. He hurried back to his flat, calling on his neighbour to collect his son. He told her what he had been told, saying he would soon be leaving, and was overjoyed to know that his father had accepted him back home.

Ishmael now had to organise his departure from the camp, which, to him, had been an open prison. First, he would tell his landlady that he would be leaving, along with his employers at the tannery, and his friend who repaired motor cars. The next day, he visited these people and told them of his plans, thanking them, at the same time, for their help and friendship. The next day, he said goodbye to his neighbours, telling them they could now have their bed back that they had kindly given him, and the remains of the furniture, with any other goods he had accumulated. Ishmael set off with the boy into the town, and took a bus to Jerusalem.

Arun and Ruth were beginning to accept their situation, and now had to decide their future. It would not be long before he was to retire. After a lot of discussion, they had made up their minds that they would leave Israel and emigrate to America, where they knew they would be welcome. Arun had thought about his father's land of Russia, which now was a totally changed and modern country, but was suspicious that it may change, as some aspects of the past still existed. The day came for his retirement. He was at the military headquarters, and was given a send-off reception, with a long-service medal of commendation for his long service to the State of Israel. Arun accepted this accolade modestly. In his heart, he was pleased and relieved he would no longer have to witness all the death and grief of the day-to-day disasters. Knowing what was happening in other parts of the world, Arun said they had made the right choice. After a few days, he arranged with Ruth to organise the sale of their house and possessions. They would make a clean start with a new life in America, the place his father had nearly decided to go from Russia.

* * *

A month had passed, and it was now the year 1999, and things were moving fast. Having sold the house and contents, Arun and Ruth would soon be leaving to a new life in America, which, to them, was the new 'Land of Opportunity'. Ruth felt a little sad; she would like to have returned to the Lebanon, the original home of her mother, Letitia, and her father, Usef. She knew this was not possible, so she had no other option but to go along with Arun. A number of weeks had passed. Now that the house had been sold, they were ready to depart, having organised their flight tickets. Ruth and Arun had said goodbye earlier that evening to their close friends, and had a special farewell for the rabbi, who had been a good friend to his father, Daniel. Setting off on a bus from Jerusalem to the airport, both were feeling apprehensive and, at the same time, hopeful.

They were nearly halfway to the airport when a mighty explosion tore into the evening air. The bus was almost totally wrecked by a roadside bomb, which had been remotely controlled. It was a scene of carnage. The army and medics were quickly on the scene, attending to the injured. After all he had been through and experienced, Arun was dead, and his wife, Ruth, was seriously injured. She was rushed to the hospital with the other casualties. It was the ultimate tragedy in the life of a family that had begun with so much promise. Ruth never reached America. After weeks in hospital, she made a good recovery, and then went back to her relatives who had taken in her father, Usef, in Lebanon, when he had been displaced from his land. Ruth, eventually, did have her wish, albeit under tragic circumstances.

* * *

This pattern of violence exists because of the lack of compassion and respect for fellow human beings. Wars and conflicts are usually started by one nation displacing another from their land and interfering in their daily life through political or religious means, or through plain greed. The situation in Palestine and Israel is an example of how a country can become a nightmare of horror and terror through each other's lack of understanding and belief, both peoples having suffered horrific persecution in the process. It is reasonable to say or assume that man is his own enemy. It is also questionable who has the answer to the truth when it comes to religious thinking, which, to some laymen, produces hatred and tension among nations. Religion and other beliefs have been questioned over the centuries. Six hundred years before Christ, the School of Sceptics doubted a god existed, or even a creator. In more modern times, Einstein, the renowned Jewish mathematician and physicist, in a letter before his death, said that all religions were, to him, childish, and God was an expression of human weakness, and the Bible a collection of honourable but primitive legends. That, of course, was the opinion of only one man, but, to many people, religious belief is something that they build their lives around.

Still, the question remains, do any of us know the truth? Ironically, Ishmael's wife, Hagar— or Deborah— unlike her biblical namesake, who was a prophetess, who dispensed judgement to the children of Israel, according to the Book of Judges— Chapter 4, Verse 4— could be said to have received judgement herself from the children of Israel, as Hagar was no prophetess, and could not have foretold her own fate.

Meanwhile, the torture, murder, and deprivation still go on throughout the world in a never-ending spiral of death. One hope came out of this ongoing quagmire of death and destruction meted out by both Palestinians and Israelis.

The good news was that Ishmael and his son, Ibrahim, were welcomed back in Jerusalem to his father, Ahmed's, house. They would now bring up his son in the family. Ishmael had also obtained employment, working in an Israeli lawyer's office, hoping, through his studies, to become a lawyer himself one day. However, the situation, despite efforts of conciliation and national appeals by many nations to obtain a fair and lasting solution, falls on deaf ears. Unless there are significant changes, the Land of Milk and Honey will, no doubt, continue to flow with blood and tears.

Lightning Source UK Ltd.
Milton Keynes UK
29 September 2010

160571UK00001B/71/P